DRUG

(Kassidy Bell Trilogy)
Book 1

Lynda O'Rourke

Copyright © 2014 Lynda O'Rourke
All rights reserved.
ISBN: 10: 1505336775

ISBN-13: 978-1505336771

First Edition Published by Ravenwoodgreys
Copyright 2014 by Lynda O'Rourke

This book is a work of fiction. The names, characters, places, and incidents are products of the writer's imagination or have been used fictitiously and are not to be construed as real. Any resemblance to persons, living or dead, actual events, locales or organisations is entirely coincidental.

This eBook is licensed for your personal enjoyment only. This eBook may not be re-sold or given away to other people. If you would like to share this book with another person, please purchase an additional copy for each recipient. If you're reading this book and did not purchase it, or it was not purchased for your use only, then please purchase your own copy. Thank you for respecting the hard work of this author.

Story Editor
Tim O'Rourke
Book cover designed by:
Tom O'Rourke
Copyedited by:
Carolyn M. Pinard
www.cjpinard.com

For Tim - Thank you for all your help and encouragement and giving me a taste over the last three years of how much fun it is to write a book – I'm now hooked on writing – love you.

For Joseph, Thomas, and Zachary – this book is a little of me that will stay with you when I'm long gone – love you all.

For Snuffy – for keeping me company while I wrote Drug.

DRUG

CHAPTER ONE

I took another look at the security guards standing by the large metal gates just over my shoulder. The place looked like a prison with its tall wire fences and security cameras. There were bars on the windows – to keep people out or in?

I shuddered.

My mind was on overdrive. I took my phone out of my pocket. A text from my friend Hannah flashed on the screen. Maybe this would take my mind off of what I had let myself in for. I'd told her over the phone late last night what I was going to do. She thought I'd lost my freaking mind – but understood my reasons. The text read:

Good luck, Kassidy, I hope all goes well. Rather you than me! When you get out of that place tomorrow come over at six. Don't forget my new address – 4 Christchurch Road. Can't wait to show you my new flat. It's gorgeous! Love ya, wouldn't wanna be ya! Hannah x

I wouldn't wanna be me either. I placed my phone back into my pocket. It was okay for Hannah, she had a good job. A job that paid well enough for her to move into some posh new development near to the marina where all the rich city-types lived. Hannah had suggested I get a job – to look in the local paper. It had to be worth a try. Four weeks ago I'd had a job. But I'd been made redundant and was now struggling to pay my rent. I was up to my eyeballs in debt. I had been scraping through – *just*. But with no job now, I was gonna sink fast. My rent was due in the next couple of days and I knew my landlord wouldn't be kind. I had to find a job, and fast.

So just two days ago, I'd sat alone at the kitchen table and flicked through the local newspaper to the job section. It didn't surprise me that I wasn't qualified for any of the available positions, unless I wanted to clean toilets or mop floors. I would if I had to, but not yet. And besides, the wage was crap. I'd never be able to pay my bills on that silly amount each month. I was about to give up when something caught my eye. A small advertisement right at the bottom of the page. The word *WANTED* stood out like a sore thumb. It wasn't a job – more like a quick fix. But it would keep me going for a few months, at least until I found something more permanent.

That's why I now stood in line. I tried to tell myself I could be doing worse things to make money – like pimping myself – or there was always the exciting prospect of cleaning those toilets and mopping floors. But I still couldn't shake that growing unease I felt.

The line suddenly moved forward. Straining to see the people in front, I think I counted nine. Are we going in now? Shit, this was it. The point of no return? Maybe I could change my mind after I'd seen what was inside? *Calm down. You'll be fine,* I told myself. If it was going to be that bad then surely all these other people in line wouldn't be doing it. Some of them looked a bit older than me, probably had more common sense than I did, so surely they wouldn't be getting themselves mixed up in something like this if it was dangerous? And besides – none of them had two heads – not that I could see!

It was at moments like this I missed my dad. Even though when he had been alive he hadn't been able to string more than a few slurred sentences together – he had still been company of a sort. So after work I would go and sit by his grave. Did he hear my sobs? Did he know the mess he had left me in because of his drinking? If he did, he didn't say so.

I was nervous. Could any amount of money be worth the anxiety I was now feeling? I tried to calm my breathing. Deep breaths in and out. In and out. In and out. It was no use – those butterflies in my stomach just wouldn't ease. My hands shook. My heart thumped. Why had I got myself into this? I could turn around right now and ask security to let me out. Tell them I'd changed my mind. But what did I have to go back to?

"Excuse me", I said, tapping the shoulder of the girl standing in front of me.

She turned around and smiled. She must have been in her early twenties.

"Yes?" she said, pulling her coat tight around her.

"Do you know what they're gonna do to us"? I asked. "That letter they sent didn't really say very much".

"All I know is that I had to turn up here at midday with my passport," she said. "I mean, I know what I've signed up for, I just don't know how it's going to be done."

"I'm feeling rather nervous," I admitted. "I'm not sure if I've made the right decision by coming here."

"Nothing bad is going to happen – these places wouldn't be allowed to exist if it was dangerous," she said.

"I guess," I shrugged. "It just doesn't look like the friendliest of places."

"What's your name? I'm Carly," she smiled.

"Kassidy Bell," I said, pulling my blonde hair from out of my face. The wind had picked up and the dark clouds threatened rain. It had been warm and sunny earlier when I'd taken the bus from town. The trip up Strangers Hill had only taken twenty minutes, but it had seemed longer with those butterflies inside my stomach starting to feel more like a flock of crows.

"Looks like we're going in," Carly said, turning and following the line.

I trailed after her, each step feeling like I had a bag of cement attached to my feet. One more glance at the gate – my escape. Doubts were running wild in my head, but I needed the money. I had to do this.

CHAPTER TWO

We were led down a corridor into a reception area. The first thing I noticed was the sterile smell, just like a hospital. The walls were blank and the floors tiled. Nothing out of place – it was all very pristine.

"Good afternoon, everyone, my name is Doctor Middleton," a guy in a white coat said. He was thin, tall, and probably in his fifties. He cleared his throat like he had something stuck in it. "If you could take a seat then I will hand you all an information sheet and consent form."

I sat down next to Carly. Even though I'd only spoken to her briefly outside, I kinda felt I could ask her for help if I needed it.

"Do you know anyone who has ever done this before?" I whispered, biting my fingernail.

"My boyfriend's brother did it once," she said, fiddling with a button on her coat.

"Really? And he was fine afterwards"? I asked, feeling a sense of relief at hearing this.

"No, he died," Carly said, shaking her head.

"You're joking!" I gasped rather too loudly. A girl with greasy black hair sitting a couple of chairs away looked over at me.

"I'm winding you up," she sniggered. "I don't know anyone who has done this, but it's got to be a good thing we're doing – think of all those people we might be helping – *saving*!"

"Is that why you volunteered? You want to help sick people?" I asked, feeling rather shallow at my own reasons for doing this.

"Of course, and let's not forget the money." She winked, elbowing me in the ribs.

I smiled. Carly was nice. A bit of a wind-up but she made me feel at ease. I was about to ask her what she needed the money for when Doctor Middleton walked past handing me a pen and two sheets of paper attached to a clipboard.

"Please take your time reading the information sheet. It explains exactly what the trial involves. The whole procedure is written very clearly for you. If you have any questions after you have read it then please feel free to ask me," Doctor Middleton smiled, handing Carly a clipboard.

"Excuse me," said a young guy at the front of the room. "What is this drug going to be used for?"

"Can I take your name?" Doctor Middleton asked, looking down at some notes he had in his hands.

"Max Landy," the guy said. "Have you tested this drug on humans before?"

"No. These are the first human trials of the drug. But I can assure you, it's going to help millions of people. The drug is designed to strengthen the immune system," Doctor Middleton explained, clearing his throat again. "The results from the initial laboratory studies show an excellent response to the drug, and now we are well and truly ready to start human testing – that is why you are all here today."

"Hey, I've signed my consent form," Max said, waving it around in the air like he was holding the winning lottery ticket.

He seemed way more desperate than me to get his hands on the £2,000 we had been promised for becoming guinea pigs overnight. But it was a lot of money. To me, anyhow.

"How much?!" Hannah had gasped, when I'd told her last night. "Who pays that kind of money just to stick a few needles in your arm? Sounds *too* good to be true if you ask me."

Well, I hadn't been asking her. I needed the money.

I watched the other volunteers to see if they were signing. I hadn't even read through the information sheet yet. Three more people stood up and handed the consent forms to Doctor Middleton. I looked back down and tried to speed-read the sentences. The first few paragraphs were about the company – *Cruor Pharma*. The second part was the *do's* and *don'ts* while in the building – the rules. I skipped through most of that. Then I got to the bit about the actual procedure. The drug – named VA20 – would be administered through a drip. All volunteers would be monitored throughout the night.

"I would like to add," Doctor Middleton started, "that you still have time to pull out of this drug trial up until you reach the ward, so please bear that in mind".

"We've signed ours," called out two young girls, passing the forms to him.

"Thank you," he said, attaching them to the clipboard he was holding. "Can you give me your names so I can tick you both off the list please?"

"Wendy Jones and May Stapleton," they answered, sitting back down.

"Are you gonna sign that form or just stare at it?" Carly asked me. "I'm ready to hand mine in but I'll wait for you if you want?"

"I haven't read it all," I said, pen hovering over the signature box – the pressure to sign making me sweat. Was I doing the right thing? Everyone else here seemed very relaxed – like they'd just signed up for a college course. No big deal.

"Just sign it," Carly cut in. "I've read it and there's nothing to worry about. You're not gonna come out of here tomorrow morning with a beard and pointed ears."

"Okay, I'll sign it," I smiled, not wanting to be the only one in the room making a fuss. I did still have time to pull out before I got to the ward after all.

Carly snatched my form, walked over to Doctor Middleton, and told him our names so he could tick us off his list. I took the moment to have a look at the other volunteers. They were all young. Five males and five females. I wondered what shit in their lives had brought them here. Did they need the money as badly as me? Was life giving them a tough ride?

"If you could all follow me please, we can head down to the consultation rooms where you will have your health check and answer a few questions," Doctor Middleton informed us, holding open the door.

"Come on, Kassidy," Carly called from across the room.

I followed the rest of the group. The place was huge. Corridor after corridor. Doctors and scientists bustling about. Upstairs and past labs.

It felt like we had been walking forever when Doctor Middleton suddenly came to a stop.

"Wait here, and when your name is called out, proceed through there," he said, pointing to a nearby door. "I'm going off to the ward now to make sure my staff are ready."

I wandered over to the window. The rain had started and the wind was blowing quite a gale. I could see the security guards outside – long raincoats and hoods pulled up tight. I counted ten, but there could've been more. The sterile rooms no longer looked bright and sparkling clean, just dark and unfriendly. The rain pelted against the window blurring my view.

"Hi, I'm Jude," a young guy with black hair said.

"Hey," I smiled, looking into his blue eyes. I hadn't seen him come over to the window. "I'm Kassidy."

"Yeah, I know," he said. "Your friend Carly told me. She said you were feeling scared. Don't worry, I've done this before and I've never had one side effect. It's quite safe."

"I'm not scared," I said, feeling my cheeks flush. "I just wasn't sure if I was doing the right thing, that's all. I don't really like hospitals – they make me a little nervous."

"Well if it makes you feel any better, this isn't really a hospital anymore – more like a huge science lab." He grinned, running his hand through his short, wavy hair.

"Okay, I'll bear that in mind when they're sticking needles into me and pumping only God knows what into my veins," I smiled, looking down at my feet.

"It's only for one night, remember. And at least we're in a group of nice people," he said. "One needle and two grand in the bank. Easy money. Oh and you get to spend a night with me! Now that's got to be worth having a needle stuck into you."

"I think the two grand seems the most appealing," I smiled, wiping the condensation from the window.

"Kassidy Bell." Someone called my name.

I looked across the room to see another doctor. She was bottle- blonde, grey roots refusing to go away, wrinkles around her eyes. She called my name again.

"Here," I said, waving my hand in the air. "It was nice chatting to you, Jude. Maybe we can talk some more on the ward."

"I would love to," he smiled, eyes twinkling.

I turned away – heart slightly racing. Not because I was about to have my health check but the thought of spending some more time with Jude was something to look forward to. He seemed cool, a bit of fun, and that was something I hadn't had for a while. Maybe this drug trial wasn't going to be as bad as I had first thought.

CHAPTER THREE

"Kassidy, have you been ill in the last week?" asked Doctor Wright, pen twitching in her hand.

"No," I said, letting my eyes wander around her office. It was very plain – just a couple of old photos of the Cruor Pharma building hanging on the walls. Classical music played quietly in the background.

"Have you ever suffered from any of these?" she asked, handing me a list of illnesses.

After a minute I placed the sheet of paper down onto her desk. "No, I've always been really healthy – my dad used to say I could drink drain water and not get ill."

Not looking up from her paperwork, Doctor Wright continued to make notes. "Really – that's nice, now let's take your temperature and blood pressure."

Hmmm, you wouldn't want to get stuck in a room with her for too long – she hardly won the award for friendliness. Bit of an old cow. I hoped it wouldn't be her fixing me up to the drip later.

"Okay, that all seems fine. Now could you stand on the scales please?" she asked, pointing behind me.

"So is Doctor Middleton in charge of all this?" I asked, standing on the cold scales.

"Nine stone and one pound," she wrote down. "Doctor Middleton is standing in for Doctor Langstone as he has been taken ill. Stand up against that wall chart so I can take your height."

I stared out through the window as she measured me. The rain still fell hard. I could see the tree branches bending over to the right – the wind must be pretty strong.

"Five foot, eight inches," Doctor Wright said. "All I need to do is take a blood sample from you and then you're ready for the ward."

"If anything goes wrong, what will happen?" I asked, chewing on my lower lip.

"Nothing will go wrong, Kassidy. We are highly trained doctors and scientists and have been doing drug trials for many years here. Hold your arm out please."

I watched the needle break the skin. A sharp sting. A pull on my arm like sucking milkshake through a straw. A small glass bottle slowly filled with my blood. Was she gonna leave me some, or did the greedy old bag want it all?

She pulled the needle out, handing me some cotton wool to hold over the small bloody hole.

"All done, you can join the others outside," she said, writing my name on the bottle of blood.

I left the room, glad to be free of Doctor Wright. She certainly didn't go out of her way to make you feel wanted. I looked for Carly. She was standing by a vending machine with another girl. I think her name was Wendy Jones. She and her friend had been pretty keen in reception to hand in their consent forms.

"Hey, Kassidy," Carly smiled. "This is Wendy."

Wendy gave me a huge smile. Her skin was masked in freckles and her bright orange hair stuck out in all directions.

"Have you two had your checks done yet?" I asked, the nerves of going to the ward beginning to creep through me again.

"Yeah," said Wendy. "My friend May hasn't come out yet – she's probably trying to get as much time as she can with Doctor Fletcher. Have you seen him? Talk about making you feel hot under the collar." She flapped her hands about in front of her face as if to cool herself down.

"No, I haven't seen him," I said, my eyes wandering around the room for Jude. He was sitting with Max, the guy who had been asking questions in reception earlier and some bald-headed bloke. Jude was good-looking with tanned skin – like a surfer. I could just picture him propped against a beach bar, surfboard in one hand and a lager in the other.

"Excuse me, everyone." Doctor Middleton had reappeared. "Before we move on to the ward please place your passports and any electronic devices into these envelopes and mark your name clearly on the front."

"Why can't we take our phones in?" Carly asked, hands on hips.

"For security reasons. What we do here isn't always appreciated by members of the public. We've had protesters turn up at the front gates before. Any film footage leaked out could put the security of Cruor Pharma in jeopardy. We like to keep our tests – our work confidential," Doctor Middleton explained.

"What about our passports? What are you going to do with them? No one's even checked mine yet," said the bald guy sitting with Jude.

"The passports are needed to verify who you are and will be kept in our safe," answered Doctor Middleton. "There is no need to worry. You will get your items back tomorrow, once you are finished on the ward."

Jude stood up and placed his mobile and passport into one of the envelopes. The rest of the group followed. I checked my phone one last time before handing it over with my passport. May had come back and was standing with her friend. She whispered behind her hand – probably telling Wendy all about Doctor Fletcher. A security guard walked in and took the envelopes away in a clear plastic bag. I checked my watch – 5 p.m. already. Where had the day gone? It was almost dark now and my stomach rumbled for dinner. Carly must have been feeling the same as she called out to Doctor Middleton.

"Do we get any dinner? I'm starving. I haven't eaten since breakfast." She held her stomach.

"A light meal has been laid on for you," smiled Doctor Middleton. He cleared his throat. "As soon as you are settled on the ward, the staff will bring it out. Now if you would all follow me, we can proceed. It's a bit of a trek I'm afraid, it's in the old part of the building, away from all the labs. The ward is only ever used now when overnight drug tests are being undertaken."

After walking in silence we stopped outside a door. A sign clearly stated that no unauthorised personnel were permitted to enter. Doctor Middleton pulled out a card and held it in front of a device. The door slid open to reveal a long corridor. Gone were the white shiny floor tiles and the sterile smell of disinfectant. A damp, musty aroma filled my nostrils as I walked along the frayed brown carpet. The fluorescent lighting overhead flickered, casting shadows along the wall. I wished I was back in my flat. I didn't like the look of this place. Alarm bells started ringing in my head. I stopped. My feet didn't want to go any further.

"Hey, are you all right?" Jude asked, staring into my eyes.

"I don't want to stay here," I whispered. "I don't like it."

"You know, I've stayed in worse hotels than this," he laughed. "Yeah, it's a bit grim but once you've had some dinner and settled in, everything will seem better. You're one night away from earning two grand. The first thing I'm gonna do when I get out of this place is buy myself a plane ticket to Canada. What about you? There must be something you really want or you wouldn't be here, Kassidy."

He was right of course. I needed to get back on my feet and keep the wolves away from my door. This was my only chance of doing that.

I sighed. "I need to pay off some debts. My dad died four months ago and left me with a lot of money problems. I don't have a job anymore so I can't pay the debts."

"There you go, see?" he said. "That's your motivation for going through with tonight. You'll be fine, I'll look after you. Come on – we need to catch up with the others."

He took hold of my hand – pulling me gently along the corridor. As we rounded a bend, I could see the group had stopped in front of some double doors. A sign above it read *Ward 2*. Almost opposite was *Ward 1*, but the doors had been locked with a padlock. There was one more door at the end of the corridor which looked like a cupboard.

"Here we are," smiled Doctor Middleton, stepping aside. "The ward has been separated into two halves. Males at one end, females at the other."

I looked at Jude. He gave me a reassuring grin like we were queuing up for a thrill ride, which he was persuading me to go on.

"Come on, Kassidy," he smiled. "You know you want to. You get a whole night with me!"

I laughed. What was I waiting for? I could do this. Tomorrow I would be walking out of here with two grand and probably signing up for my next drug trial. I took a deep breath and stepped into Ward 2.

CHAPTER FOUR

I felt like I'd stepped back in time. Images of Victorian hospitals came to mind. It was so different to the rest of the building. Old, cold, and grubby. Cracked floor tiles and barred windows. The beds had seen better days too. I bet I wouldn't get a good night's sleep on any of them. The only thing that brought me back to 2014 was the modern equipment that had been set up beside each bed. Drips!

"Take the bed next to mine," Carly said, patting the mattress. She'd already plonked herself down. The bed creaked like it couldn't take her weight. Wendy and May had taken two beds opposite, and the girl I had seen earlier in reception with the greasy black hair had taken the bed nearest to the door. At the far end of the ward, the guys had already picked where they were sleeping. Two nurses walked in handing out hospital gowns.

"Oh no, we haven't got to wear *those* things, have we?" Wendy asked. "They never fit properly – your arse always hangs out the back."

I screwed my nose up as the nurse handed me one. I tried to remember what underwear I was wearing. Thank God it wasn't a thong.

"It's only for one night, my dear," the nurse said, handing the last hospital gown to Carly.

I looked down the ward to see Jude holding his gown up and laughing with the other guys. Well at least they had to suffer the embarrassment as well.

"I'm Nurse Jones, and I will be looking after you through the night," smiled the nurse who had handed me the gown. "Dinner will be brought round in a few moments, and once you've all eaten, you will need to put on the gowns. The doctors will soon come and hook you up to the drips."

"Does that mean we can't move about?" I asked. "What if I need to go to the loo?"

"The drips are mobile, so you can walk about," she smiled. "They are a little cumbersome, so you will need to be careful not to pull them over or knock the tube from out of your arm. If you do need the bathroom, it's just through that door." She pointed to the opposite end of the ward.

The lights flickered and hummed throwing the room into darkness for just a split second. I could still hear rain pelting against the window and the howl of the wind. What a night to be stuck in this place. The doors swung open and two members of staff wheeled in trolleys loaded with covered plates. They were dressed differently from the doctors and nurses I had seen. They looked more like porters of some kind. One of them looked really old. Perhaps they had a geriatric ward here somewhere.

"Food at last," Carly grinned, making herself comfortable on the bed. She pulled the mobile table toward her.

"Sandwiches or soup?" the old guy asked, staring at me. His I.D. badge was pinned to his blue tabard. His name, Fred Butler, was engraved across the badge.

"Soup," I said, propping myself up against the pillows.

He placed a bowl down on my table and shuffled toward Carly. I lifted the lid covering the bowl. Steam poured out. The smell of the chicken soup made my stomach rumble and I tucked in. I was starving. It was quiet for a few minutes while we ate. Everyone seemed content now they had food.

"What do you need the money for, Carly?" I asked, eating the last of the soup.

"I want to visit my boyfriend. He's living in Australia at the moment. He's got a job out there," she said, licking her fork clean. "I haven't seen him for six months."

"Wendy and I are going to travel across Europe," May joined the conversation. "And when we run out of money, we'll probably do something like this again – just to keep us going."

"What do you think of Jude?" Carly asked, looking at me. "I think he likes you."

"He seems like a nice guy. Very good at putting your mind at ease," I said. "I nearly walked out of here but Jude persuaded me to stay."

"I bet he did," Carly winked.

"Wait till you see Doctor Fletcher," giggled May. "He'll get your heart racing."

"You're too young for him," teased Wendy, "he won't be interested in you."

"I'm nearly twenty," May pouted. "I'm not some silly schoolgirl."

I stood up and walked over to the window. There wasn't much to see now that it was dark – just the distant lights of the town twinkling through the rain. I wish it was me who was going travelling. Maybe when I'd paid off my debts and found a job? Perhaps I could save up some money and...who was I kidding? I was never gonna find a job that would pay well enough for that.

"Not having second thoughts again, are you?" Jude suddenly whispered in my ear.

"No," I smiled, turning to face him. That was the second time today he'd crept up behind me. "I was just daydreaming. Don't think we're gonna get much sleep in here tonight, do you?"

"Not if I'm with you I won't," he grinned – pushing his luck again. "Do you fancy hanging out with me once you've been hooked up to the drips? I'm sure there's plenty for us to do – to while away the hours."

I could feel my face blush. I looked away. Was he just playing or did he mean what I thought he meant? I didn't really know why he was bothering with me. After all – he would be off to Canada tomorrow. Surely he wasn't after a one night stand! Not in this place. Perhaps he was just one of those guys with a permanent hard-on?

"We can hang out," I said, "as long as you make room for me *and* my drip. What are the other guys like? I haven't spoken to any of them, yet."

"Max is cool – he's the one in the bed next to mine. See that guy with the brown hair – Simon?" he asked. "He's a bit of an idiot, only wants the money so he can gamble it away – what a waste. I haven't spoken much to the other two, but the one with the pierced lip is Howard, and the bald headed guy is James".

"Hey, you two," Carly called over to us. "Nurse Jones says we have to get changed – the doctors will be here in five minutes."

"Guess I'd better get going – make sure you put on your best dress when you come and visit me tonight," Jude winked.

"Will do. I think I've got a rather revealing gown I could throw on," I laughed, walking back over to my bed.

I pulled the curtain round. This was it. I was soon to have some untested drug travelling around my body and although it had been the one thing that had bothered me the most – now I felt surprisingly calm. Even the grim surroundings didn't worry me anymore. I slipped the gown on and tried to tie the back, hoping I could shut as much of the gap up as possible.

"Pssst, Kassidy – can I come in?" Carly asked, poking her head around the curtain. "Do you think you can tie my gown up? The gap must be as wide as a freaking motorway!"

I laughed. "Only if you do mine up for me. There you go, I've done it."

"Thanks," she said, tying me up. "Do you want me to open this curtain?"

I nodded my head. "Might as well. I want to see what's going on."

I climbed onto my bed. Doctor Middleton walked onto the ward with Doctor Wright and who I guessed was Doctor Fletcher. He was *very* good looking. May was giggling again at the sight of him. He had short black hair, clear blue eyes, and he *definitely* worked out. The doctors were no longer in their white coats but now in scrubs. Nurse Jones trailed behind them pushing a trolley with surgical items. There was a large box underneath which read VA20. The mystery drug. I wondered what could be in it. The girl with the black greasy hair on the bed by the door suddenly spoke up. It was the first time I had heard her speak.

"Can you tell me what's in that drug? It isn't going to kill me, is it?" she asked, slipping a greasy strand of hair behind her ears.

A bit late to be asking that now. Was she getting cold feet? Her brown eyes flicked from one doctor to the next.

"It's highly classified. I can't divulge what is in it," Doctor Middleton said, clearing his throat. "But I can assure you that it has been passed by the MHRA and all the ethical bodies. VA20 has been cleared for human trials."

"But you don't know if it's going to kill me, do you?" she said, lips trembling.

"She has got a point you know," Carly winked at me. "We are putting our bodies and health on the line here."

"And *we* are paying you for that," Doctor Wright said. "You have all had the chance to pull out."

"Well I'm staying," Wendy said. "What about you, Kassidy?"

The girl on the bed had made me feel a little unnerved with her questions. I didn't know what was in this drug or what it would do to me. If someone had offered me heroin or crack I would tell them where to stick it. But here I was now, willing to take a drug that I'd never heard of, just for money. But I had to do this. Those final payment demand letters from the debt collectors flashed through my mind. At least if anything went wrong we were surrounded by medical staff.

"I'm staying," I said, determined to see this night through. People were always having drips stuck in them. Okay, so it wasn't untested drugs they were getting pumped with but still… all medicines had been tested on someone and I'd never heard of any incidents where it had gone horribly wrong. That kind of shit would make the news.

"Fine, I'm staying too," said Carly, crossing her arms.

"And you?" Doctor Middleton asked the girl who had caused all the upset.

She nodded her head slowly as if still unsure. Scratching her scalp with her black-painted fingernails, she pulled the blanket up under her chin.

"Nurse Jones, could you start by applying the cream to each patient please," said Doctor Fletcher.

He lifted the box from under the trolley placing it on a table with a thump. May couldn't take her eyes off Doctor Fletcher. Every time he bent over she was getting a good look at his arse, then fanning herself like the view was too much. I smiled. It was like being back at school with my mates – sitting together and getting all giggly at one of the young male teachers everyone fancied.

Nurse Jones came over and asked me to hold out my arm.

"This is just to numb the area where the needle will go in," she smiled, squeezing the white cream onto the crook of my elbow. "All done. Doctor Fletcher is looking after you tonight, so you're in safe hands."

"I'm glad it's not Doctor Wright," I whispered. "She seems really angry."

"No, no, that's just her way. She likes to get the job done efficiently, that's all," Nurse Jones said, pulling off her latex gloves.

"Do you always work on this ward for drug trials?" I asked, leaning back on my pillow.

"It's the first one I've done on Ward 2," she said. "And it's the first one I've stayed the whole night for. Normally, I just help set up the patients and I'm usually done by 8 p.m. But the doctors needed the extra staff so I'm here until the morning. I used to work at *Cruor Pharma's* sister company but they've downsized recently and asked me to move here. It was the only way of keeping my job. Anyway, I can't stand here talking all night or I'll be in trouble," she said, walking away.

I looked down the ward. The guys had all had the anaesthetic cream applied and were now waiting for the drips to be hooked up. It seemed they had the joy of Doctor Wright looking after them for the night. Jude gave me a little wave and a thumbs down at Doctor Wright while she had her back turned to him. I responded with a thumbs up for Doctor Fletcher and a big smile.

"Ouch! That hurts a bit," Wendy said, holding her arm.

Doctor Middleton was inserting a needle into her vein. Nurse Jones held the drip stand steady.

"Just try and relax," Doctor Middleton said. "This is always the hardest part if you struggle. There you go, Wendy. That wasn't too bad now, was it?"

"That cream didn't do much to numb the pain," she moaned. "It felt more like a hose pipe being inserted than a needle."

Doctor Middleton moved on to May. She sat with a scowl, annoyed that Doctor Fletcher wasn't looking after her. You could see the envy in her eyes as he finished with Carly and moved over to me. This was my first chance to get a close up of him. He looked fit. Eyes seductive and lips that could set your skin on fire.

He looked at his paperwork and wrote something down. "Kassidy, could you rest your arm out on the bed for me – like this," he said, gently taking my arm, his fingers lightly sliding over my skin. His blue eyes concentrating at the task in hand. I looked down at the plastic tube.

"Don't look, just lay back and relax," he whispered. "There's nothing to worry about. I won't hurt you."

I did as I was told. My eyes closed and I breathed a deep sigh. Doctor Fletcher was good. With a bedside manner like that, I would let him stick tubes in me all night.

I felt his fingers brush the side of my face. I opened my eyes to find him staring down at me.

"The tube's in," he said. "I'm going to attach the unit of VA20 now."

He held up a black bag its contents hidden. My heart thumped. Last minute nerves. He must have noticed the sudden look of panic in my eyes. Taking my hand, he calmly stroked my fingers.

"I'm going to be here all night, Kassidy," he said. "I will check on you every hour to see if you are all right."

He looked over his shoulder, making sure no one could hear him. Then, he bent over me and whispered, "You make sure you tell me if you're not feeling right. Don't tell Doctor…"

"Have you finished, Doctor Fletcher? The other volunteers are all done," Doctor Middleton appeared beside the bed. "Nurse Jones needs a hand adjusting an I.V. pole."

Doctor Fletcher nodded his head and walked away. That was weird. What doctor was he referring to? I looked up at Doctor Middleton. He was checking the bag of VA20. He smiled as if satisfied. Then, looking down at me, he said, "You can walk about if you want but please be careful not to knock the cannula out from your arm – it's very easy to pull the needle out if you catch it on something."

"How long will the drip be in me?" I asked, looking at the brown fluid flowing through the plastic tube.

"It should take two to three hours and then the rest of the night will be spent checking to see what reactions you have to the drug," he said, walking away.

I looked about the ward. Doctor Fletcher must have left. Carly swung her legs over the side of her bed and sat down beside me.

"Well that was okay," she smiled. "I've no idea what's in VA20, but I'm feeling all right."

I hadn't even thought about how I felt but now that she'd mentioned it – I was feeling okay too. Almost like a surge of energy flowing through me.

"This drug would be great for hangovers," I smiled. "In fact, who needs booze when you have VA20?"

I got up. Holding on to my drip, I pulled it alongside me. Had I just earnt the easiest two grand ever? Or was it all *too* good to be true?

CHAPTER FIVE

"Are you okay?" I asked the greasy-haired girl as she sat with her legs pulled up to her chin. "You looked a little freaked out a while ago."

She shrugged. "I got a bad feeling, that's all. This place has a nasty vibe, can't you feel it?"

"It's pretty creepy but I guess it's because we're in the old part of the building. Doctor Middleton said it only gets used for overnight trials."

"No, it's more than that," she said. "I can sense it. That other ward is full of something dark and evil."

This girl seemed pretty troubled. I thought I was the one getting stressed about this place but she could win awards for an overactive imagination. She looked like she behaved – weird and dark. Black makeup around her eyes and on her lips. She was probably into ghosts and the occult.

"What's your name?" I asked, sitting on the end of her bed. "I'm Kassidy."

"You can call me Raven," she said. "I don't like my real name – it's disgusting."

"What is it?" I asked, trying to hide the smile that threatened to show itself. What a strange girl. Was she even mentally stable?

"Like I'm gonna tell *you*," she said, snatching hold of her drip. "I'm going to the toilet." She stomped away toward the bathroom dragging her drip in her fist like a microphone stand that a rock star might use.

"Hey, I thought you were going to join me on *my* bed – not *hers*!" said Jude, pulling his drip behind him. He looked funny standing there with his gown on. "What do you think – sexy, huh?" he winked, spinning around.

"Nice gap at the back," I laughed, glad to be talking to Jude and not Raven.

"Nurse Jones has brought a portable radio in, fancy listening to some tunes?" he said. "There's not much else to do. The others are sitting down there."

"Sounds good to me," I smiled, making sure the needle in my arm was still in place. It was feeling a little uncomfortable.

Money's too tight to mention, by Simply Red was playing quietly. As if I didn't need reminding about my cash flow or lack of it, I thought. Carly, Wendy, and Max were having a game of cards. Chase the Ace. I hadn't played that for years. They had all positioned their drips neatly around Max's bed. May was perched on the edge of a metal chair, picking nail polish from her toes. The gambling guy – Simon who Jude had pointed out earlier was reading a book, and

Howard and James had gone to sleep. The lights sputtered again throwing the room into darkness for a couple of seconds. I sat down next to Jude on his bed, putting my feet up. What a strange scenario to be in. A bunch of strangers in hospital gowns huddled up together in some rundown ward. All of us in it for the money. What would my dad think if he could see me now? Probably plan on what booze he could buy with the two grand.

    I could hear him slurring – *Go get your old man a bottle of whisky and some cans.*

    I sighed. I had spent all of my childhood looking after my dad – clearing up after all of his binge-drinking sessions – pretending to the outside world that everything in my life was just fine. Smiling when all I wanted to do was fall apart. I had managed to keep most of my friends away from my home – too embarrassed by my dad's pissed-up behaviour. We had lived on benefits – my dad unfit to work, and of course what little money we did get went on the bottle. Growing up had been hard – lonely and now that he was gone – life seemed harder. I never knew what had driven him to drink – what haunted him behind those bloodshot, watery eyes, but whatever it had been had left me in a whole lot of mess.

"This is nice and cosy," Jude stirred me from my thoughts. "We could all play a game of strip poker."

"It wouldn't take very long," May sniggered. "There's not much to take off."

"All the better," Jude winked, shifting closer to me. He was definitely a flirt but I liked him. He wasn't the kind of guy you would want to settle down with, but if it was fun you were after then he'd be your man.

"Why are you going to Canada?" I asked. "Are you visiting someone or just travelling?"

"Just travelling," he said. "I get bored staying in the same place for too long. I mean, there's not much to do in this town, just the usual bars and shops. I want some fun. I can't put up with this dull, dreary existence any longer. I need to see new places, find new people, and just mess around."

"Yeah, Holly Tree must be the most boring place on Earth," Wendy said. "You should take the two grand tomorrow and come travelling with us, Kassidy."

I nodded my head. My mind drifting off to the possibilities of starting a whole new life for myself once tonight was over. Living the free life of a traveller. After all, the only ties I had here were debt related. The only family member I had now was my uncle, and he lived miles away. I hadn't seen him since I was little.

"It would be good to have some fun, I haven't been on holiday for ages," I smiled, remembering the school holiday to France and how Hannah's parents had paid for me to go. I was only nineteen – too young to be saddled with these money problems. I could just grab some things from home and jump on a plane – never come back. But what about my dad's grave? Who would visit him? Who would talk to him? No one. He had left me but I couldn't leave him – not yet anyway. I blinked away the tears that were suddenly threatening. No, I had to stay.

"You could come to Canada with me," Jude said, staring into my eyes.

"Thanks, I'd love to go to Canada but I can't," I said, faking a smile. "I need to find a job and just get my life back on track. The last four months have been hell. I lost my dad *and* lost my job. I've got nothing except the two grand coming to me tomorrow."

"I'm staying," said Max. "I work in a bookstore along the high street. I'm trying to save up some money so I can buy my own place instead of renting. We could always meet up for a drink, Kassidy, if you're at a loose end? We could chat about this place and reminisce."

I smiled. Max seemed like a gentle kind of guy. Blonde hair tied up in a ponytail with green, happy eyes.

"I'd love to," I said, trying to pull my gown down over my knees. Another song started to play on the radio. It was *Hurt* by Christina Aguilera.

The doors to the ward opened and Doctor Fletcher walked in. The atmosphere in the room changed, like he had brought the storm outside with him. His moody blue eyes searched me out.

"Kassidy, it's time to check up on you," he said, waiting beside my bed.

Had it been an hour already? I walked slowly pulling my drip beside me. Doctor Fletcher stared, his eyes searching mine – like he was expecting to see me do something. I felt uncomfortable. Those gentle eyes from earlier now seemed piercing and menacing. He helped me up onto the bed and pulled the curtain around us.

"How are you feeling?" he asked, sitting on the edge of my bed.

"Fine," I shrugged.

He wrote some notes on my file. Then pulling out a small torch he said, "I want to have a look at your eyes."

He gently pulled my lower lids down and shone the light into my pupils, his face so close to mine I could feel his breath against my skin, the smell of his aftershave wafting up my nose. "I'd like you to open your mouth please," he said, cupping my chin in his hand.

He placed his finger on my lips and slowly pushed it in against my gums, working it around my mouth. What the hell was he looking for? Was he expecting my teeth to fall out?

"Lean forward, Kassidy," he said, removing his finger from my mouth. "I want to listen to your heart."

He untied the top string of my gown and loosened it around my shoulders. Using a stethoscope, he slid his hand down beneath my gown. I shuddered. The metal was cold. But his touch against my chest was making me *hot*! May was right about Doctor Fletcher – he was getting my blood pumping.

"Breathe in, breathe out," he said, eyes melting into mine. I could only stare back – mesmerized by his gaze, excited by his touch.

He pulled his hand out. The trance-like state I had been in – broken.

"Let's take your temperature," he said, pulling out a thermometer from his pocket.

Where was he gonna stick that? Right now I really didn't care. But I was pretty sure the thermometer would burst into flames if he put it anywhere near me.

"What's making you smile, Kassidy?" he asked, sliding the thermometer between my lips.

I hadn't realised I was sitting there with a daft grin on my face because of the dirty thoughts I was having about him. Get a grip! He wouldn't be interested in me anyway – he was probably married to some lucky cow – my eyes drifted down to his left hand – no wedding ring.

He removed the thermometer and sat waiting for my reply.

"I... I... don't know." I looked down at my hands. *Please just go now. I need to bury my head under the pillow and die.*

Doctor Fletcher stood up. His eyes glimmered – like there was a smile behind them. Did he know what I'd been thinking? I hoped not.

"Lean forward, Kassidy, and I'll tie you back up," he said, getting behind me.

I felt his fingertips touch my shoulders. His muscular body pressed against my back. This was *too* much.

"Remember, I want you to let me know if you feel unwell. Even if it's just slight," he said, lifting my arm and checking the cannula. "You don't need to tell anyone else other than me, especially not the other volunteers. I don't want their results influenced by yours. Oh, and it's really late, so you should be thinking about getting some sleep instead of messing around with the guys."

He opened the curtain, and his eyes told me he disapproved.

"I haven't been messing around," I said. "I've just been talking, *that's all*. It didn't say on your list of rules that I couldn't talk with the opposite sex."

"It's a hospital ward, Kassidy, not a nightclub," he suddenly glared, then turned his back on me.

What was *his* problem? I felt like I was back at school. One minute he was close to touching me up – which I didn't mind – and now he was treating me like a child.

Doctor Wright and Doctor Middleton walked in. She looked as moody as ever. She breezed past the end of my bed heading toward the back of the ward. Doctor Middleton stopped beside Raven's bed.

"How are you feeling?" he asked, checking the bag of VA20.

"I feel sick," she glared. "That shit's poisoning me!"

She clawed at the cannula like it was irritating her. Doctor Middleton grabbed her hand and pulled it away.

"Now, now, it's not poisoning you," he said. "Let me check you over."

"I've changed my mind, I don't want this crap swimming around my body," she hissed. "It's not right, it's bad."

Doctor Middleton struggled to hold her arms still. She lashed out with her legs, just missing him.

"Nurse Jones!" he shouted. "I need your help. Doctor Fletcher, bring me a sedative."

Nurse Jones came rushing through the doors. She grabbed one of Raven's arms and held it down while Doctor Middleton fought to keep the other under control.

Jude, Carly, and Max had stood up to see what all the fuss was about. I got off my bed and joined them.

"What happened?" asked Carly. "Why did she start freaking out?"

"I don't know, she says she's being poisoned," I whispered. "She keeps shouting that the drug is bad."

"Well, obviously it's not," said Jude. "We're all fine. I feel great, don't you?"

"Nothing wrong with me," shrugged Carly. "You feel okay, don't you, Max?"

"A bit sleepy I guess, but yeah – I'm cool," he smiled. "I'm not feeling any urges to start attacking the doctors. Do you think she's seen something that we haven't? I don't mean paranormal – just something not quite right about this place."

"It's just her," Jude said. "She's weird. I tried talking to her earlier when she was stressing out. I thought I'd put her mind at ease but I guess I didn't do a good enough job of it".

"Calm down, Raven," said Nurse Jones. "You're just getting yourself all worked up."

Doctor Fletcher rushed past – syringe grasped in his hand. He knelt on the bed and pushed the needle into her arm. She tensed up and then relaxed.

"Max, Jude," Doctor Wright yelled. "Return to your beds please. I need to check you both."

"See you soon," smiled Jude, squeezing my hand, "gonna spend some time with Wright, maybe I can get her to smile." He walked away with Max, his blue boxer shorts poking through the gap of his hospital gown.

"Do you think she's okay? I mean, do you think she's just freaking out or do you think it's the drug affecting her?" I looked at Carly.

"It's not the drug. I think she's had a panic attack," Carly said, checking that her gown was still tied tight.

I turned to see May and Wendy walking back to their beds, wheeling their drips beside them.

"Hey, Kassidy," whispered May. "Has the freak stopped freaking yet?"

"She's calmed down," I said. "I've never seen anyone lose it like that before. I feel a bit stressed out myself."

"Wendy, I'd like you to lie down on the bed please so I can check you over," said Doctor Middleton. He pulled the curtain around the bed.

I looked over at Raven. She was drifting in and out of sleep. The sedative must be working. I crept up beside her.

"Raven, can you hear me?" I asked, tapping her hand softly. "Are you okay now?"

She opened her eyes and stared at me. Her greasy black hair lay across her face.

"We're all gonna die," she mumbled, closing her eyes again.

Looking out the window, I wondered what the sedative had had in it. But then again, she didn't need a sedative to come out with crazy ramblings. The sky suddenly lit up with a flash of lightning and I caught a glimpse of the car park below. It was flooded with rain. The security guards were still patrolling the grounds. I wouldn't want to do that job – mind you – they probably wouldn't want to do what I was doing. Another flash of lightning sent the ward into darkness. Turning, I gasped. I could just make out Raven in the gloom. She was sitting up – her eyes staring wide at me.

"Get out of here," she hissed then fell back against her pillow, eyes shut.

My heart thumped. She was really scaring me now. I grabbed my drip and hurried back to my bed, stumbling as I went. Two strong hands suddenly gripped me about my waist.

"The lights will come back on in a minute, you need to stay in bed."

It was Doctor Fletcher. He held me tight as I blindly tried to find my way across the ward.

"I've got you," he whispered.

I could feel his breath against my neck, his fingers stroking my flesh through the thin fabric of my gown. The ward suddenly lit up. The overhead lights stuttered and buzzed like they were choking up something. I turned around to find Doctor Fletcher had gone. I shook my head. Had I just imagined him being there? Had Raven really told me to get out? I looked at the bag of VA20. What the hell was in it? Acid? Was I tripping? I got under the blanket – goose bumps covering my skin.

CHAPTER SIX

The ward was silent. I had been lying on my bed for a while now watching Raven from beneath the cover of my blanket, wondering if she was gonna leap up and attack me. Doctor Fletcher kept creeping into my head with his *hot-cold* approach. My mind was buzzing.

The ward was still. The silence swamping me. I didn't like it. I lived in the middle of Holly Tree. The town was always noisy, but somehow it comforted me – made me feel like I wasn't alone, like I was safe. But here I felt like I was the only one in existence.

Carly had been the first to fall asleep, soon followed by Wendy and May. I wasn't sure if Raven was sleeping or whether she was just *out of it* but I sure wasn't going to try and wake her – not after last time.

A cream curtain had been pulled across the ward blocking my view of the guys.

"*It's for privacy.*" Doctor Wright had frowned at us.

I couldn't hear any noise coming from that end of the ward so I assumed they had all fallen asleep. The lights had been dimmed, not that it did anything to stop the flickering flashes every few minutes. I sat up. The tube sticking in my arm was stinging. I wanted to scratch the hell out of it. It looked sore and felt sticky. Maybe I could look for Nurse Jones. She might be able to put something on it?

I took hold of the metal drip stand. This *thing* was becoming a real bind, dragging it everywhere with me. I would be glad to see the back of it. I moved slowly toward the doors. The wheels on my drip squeaked. Stepping out into the corridor, a chill draught touched my skin. I shivered. There was no one around. My eyes fell upon the padlocked doors of Ward 1.

There's something dark and evil in there... Raven's earlier *freak-out* played on my mind.

I touched the door. Nothing! Shaking my head, I continued to move slowly up the corridor. I reached the bend. Poking my head around the corner, I could see the door which led back into the modern part of the building. There was no point going up there. I would need some kind of security card to activate the door. That only left me with the cupboard I had seen earlier, and I was pretty sure that Nurse Jones wouldn't be sitting in there.

I headed back toward the ward. It was freezing. I kept getting that feeling of being watched – hidden eyes burning through my skin. I sped up a bit – the wheels on my drip squeaking faster. The urge to check over my shoulder was *too* much to ignore. I turned, half expecting to see someone coming at me with a knife, but the corridor was empty. *Get a grip, Kassidy. You've been listening to Raven too much.* I took a few deep breaths, my heart calming. I reached for the doors. A hand gripped me by the wrist pulling me round.

I gasped. "Get off of m…" It was Doctor Fletcher. He pulled me toward him.

"What are you doing out here?" he whispered, his grip loosening. "You should be in bed asleep."

"I was looking for Nurse Jones, my arm hurts," I said, trying to pull free of his grip. "Where did you come from? You weren't behind me when I checked only seconds ago."

"Show me," he said, ignoring my question. "I thought I'd told you to only tell *me* if there was something wrong."

"It's just sore, no big deal," I said. "Surely Nurse Jones can fix me up with some cream – or does she need to be a doctor to do that?"

Blanking me again, he held my arm up. There seemed to be a glimmer of concern showing in his eyes. He put his hand over my forehead.

"You feel a bit hot," he said. "Let's get you back to bed and then I'll get you something for your arm."

"I can manage," I said, releasing his hand away from around my waist. I wasn't gonna let him touch me up again and then speak to me like I was a child.

I stormed through the doors to Ward 2. Who did he think he was? This wasn't freaking school.

"Kassidy, stop making so much noise, you'll wake everyone up," he said, stopping me dead in my tracks.

"Do you get some kind of kick in telling me what to do? I'm nineteen not thirteen," I hissed. "How old are you, twenty-five? Just because you're older doesn't mean you get to order me about."

Doctor Fletcher's lips curled up slightly at my outburst.

"Twenty-six, Kassidy," he smiled. "And while I'm your doctor you will do as I say. It's for your own good. Now, while I go and get some cream, how about you get into bed, and calm down."

"Whatever," I said.

I pulled the blanket back and climbed in. When I looked up, Doctor Fletcher had gone. Where had he come from earlier in the corridor? He couldn't have come through the door leading from the main building. I would have heard him.

Maybe he was in the cupboard with Nurse Jones – now that wouldn't surprise me.

I lay back on my pillow, eyelids feeling droopy. The silence was back again and swallowed me up as I fell asleep.

Voices drifted through the ward. My eyelids refused to open any further than a fraction. My brain refused to kick-start into first gear. Someone seemed pretty rattled out in the corridor.

"The trial should end. It will only finish like all the other ones."

It was Doctor Fletcher. A small spark of brain activity told me so. I continued to lay still – too tired to even shut my mouth which hung open. A wet patch of dribble had stuck the pillowcase to my cheek.

"We will continue. None of the volunteers are showing any bad reactions to the drug. A few have had a rise in temperature, *that's all*."

"That is exactly what happened last time," said Doctor Fletcher. "Who knows what they will be like in an hour's time."

"We will deal with them like we did the others if the situation arises. This is the closest we have got, why throw it all away now?" said Doctor Middleton.

"Maybe Doctor Fletcher is right. How many more times can we get away with doing this before someone comes looking?" said Doctor Wright.

"We have dealt with people sticking their noises in before, remember?" said Doctor Middleton.

I wanted to sit up, but my body refused. Was I just tired or was I feeling ill? The voices in the corridor faded away into a distant murmur until silence wrapped itself around me. My eyelids fell shut again.

CHAPTER SEVEN

I sat up. A noise had disturbed me. I was disorientated. Hot and sweaty. The rain still hit the windows in stormy gusts. Wind howled through the building – the walls shuddered from its strength.

My eyes moved slowly across the ward. Had I been dreaming? The state of my blanket said *nightmare*. It hung half off the bed, pillow flung across the ward. My arm hurt, the crook of my elbow black. That was one hell of a bruise.

The noise came again. I jumped. My heart quickened.

Silence.

I looked at the nearly deflated bag of VA20 still dripping its dark contents down the tube. This was one drug I would be staying well and truly clear of when it got to the open market.

A moan came from the end of the ward. My rational side tried to convince me it was just one of the guys having a nightmare or maybe they were feeling ill.

It came again. Retching and moaning. May and Carly sat up.

"What the freaking hell is that?" whispered Carly, her eyes wide.

May pulled her blanket up tight around her throat – knees up against her chest.

"I'm not sure but it's scaring the shit out of me," I murmured. "Do you think we should go and check? I mean, it sounds like someone is really ill."

We looked at each other. Fear spread across our faces.

"I'm not going through there," whispered May, shaking her head.

"Me neither," muttered Carly. "That doesn't sound human."

I slipped off the bed, tiptoeing toward the curtain, trying to keep my drip from squeaking. Fear raced through my body in contractions. My hand shook as I lifted my arm, reaching out for the curtain. I gasped in air as I pinched the fabric between my thumb and forefinger.

"Don't do it," hissed May, her blanket now just below her eyes.

I hesitated, my arm stretching out toward the curtain then dropping back down. The sudden sound of wheels squeaking from the other side of the curtain froze my blood. Someone was on the move.

I took a step back. Carly had left her bed and was now cowering behind me – I nearly fell over her. The sound of gagging got louder.

Another groan and then wet splatters peppering the floor tiles.

Silence.

"Someone's been sick that's all," I said, stepping forwards and snatching at the curtain.

A shadow moved behind the fabric. A high-pitched wail flooded the ward. Something hit the curtain. A trail of wet, red stuff, slipped down the material, falling to the floor. I looked down. A lump of bloodied flesh lay in a pool of red liquid. Another moan seeped through the fabric. Blood sprayed the curtain like rain falling on canvas.

Raven started screaming. She clambered off her bed bringing her drip crashing down. The radio we had listened to earlier came spinning out at speed from beneath the curtain hitting Wendy's bed and turning on. *Sweet Dreams* by The Eurythmics blasted through the ward. The room erupted into sheer panic. I could hear Jude shouting. The curtain came down – Max came stumbling through, slipping in the pool of blood.

"*Get out!* Get the hell out of here!" he screamed, scrambling out of the blood puddle.

I froze to the spot. James, who had fallen asleep before everyone else, was bent over Howard. His nails were hooked into Howard's skin and shredding the flesh from his chest. Long strips of bloodied muscle hung from James's mouth as he rammed it full of flesh. His skin was like a giant bruise – rotten, decaying like it was gonna fall from his bones. He gagged, drowning on the chewed-up flesh. Bubbles of clotted blood burst around his lips.

Jude had ripped his drip free and was now using it like a baseball bat trying to ward off Simon. He swung it through the air crashing it into the side of Simon's head. Blood splattered up the walls like a car splashing through puddles. Simon didn't fall or even stumble. He jumped up the wall, scurrying along it like a crab. I stood like a statue, unable to move, unable to believe what my eyes were seeing.

"Get up, Wendy!" May screamed, tugging on her friend's arm.

Wendy didn't move. She lay still. Her eyes clouded with swirls of red liquid – veins packed with black lumps pulsed under her skin.

"Leave her!" shouted Max over the din of the radio. "She's not right. She's changing!" He tried to drag May away but his blood-covered hands slipped from her wrist.

"Wendy, please!" screeched May, shaking her friend by the shoulders. "We have to get out of here."

I looked in horror as Howard came crawling across the floor toward me, gown ripped open, a trail of blood and body parts dragging behind him. His mouth stretched open in a hideous grin. How was he still alive? He snapped his arm up, grabbing my ankles with his bony hands. I toppled back, landing on my arse, bringing the drip down with me. I tried to pull away, my hands slipping on the wet tiles. He pulled himself up over my legs using my gown for grip. I could feel his hot, wet innards sliding up my skin as my gown soaked up his blood. I couldn't move my legs from under him. I was trapped.

"Get the fuck off of me!" I screamed, pushing him hard in the face with the flat of my hands. His paper-thin skin felt like mush – like custard with a skin formed over it.

He snapped his jaws at me, sharp teeth sticking out from bloodied gums. I looked about, trying to find someone to help me. Carly was hiding under my bed, her face covered in tears.

"Carly, get him off me," I pleaded.

He pulled himself up my body, gripping my shoulders. One more move and we'd be face to face. He let out a snigger – blood popped from his nostrils like a punctured abscess. The smell of old, meaty vomit suffocating me.

Carly shook her head. She lay on her side, cradling her legs up against her chest.

"*Please!*" I screamed. I felt Howard sink his teeth into my stomach. "He's gonna fucking eat me."

Blood soaked my face like a wave hitting a cliff. I tried to wipe it from my eyes – choking as it gushed down my throat. It was May's blood. I saw her falling toward me, her throat ripped open. She landed on top of Howard – pinning me down even more – knocking the air from my lungs. I gasped. Then Wendy sprang from her bed – gown drenched in blood. She threw herself onto May and tore into her face, ripping the flesh from her cheek. I gagged at the deep, bloodied hole that gapped open in the side of May's face – her tongue poked through it – flapping about like a fish out of water. A wet chewing noise filled my ears as Wendy chomped down onto a mouthful of flesh – it swung from her chin like runny jelly. She pulled at May's body with her black-veiny hands until it had rolled off Howard and me. I gulped down lungfuls of air.

Howard snatched at my hair, yanking on clumps of it. He chuckled, writhing his body against mine, ripping tufts from my scalp.

"Blood," he grinned, piercing the side of my face with his nails and raking them down my cheek. He shoved his fingers into his mouth and sucked them clean like a ravenous animal.

"*Help me!*" I screamed, punching my fists into his face. I couldn't breathe, Howard's weight crushing my body – exhaustion slowing me down.

I saw Jude standing on his bed, Raven screaming behind him. Simon still crawled across the walls – lumps of his rotten flesh falling from his bones. He snatched at Raven's hair. She ducked as Jude swung his drip, knocking Simon from the wall.

"*Jude!*" I screamed. He didn't hear me – the music blaring out from the radio was too loud. "*Jude!*"

He turned and saw me. Howard had reached my face – his black tongue shot from his mouth, stretching – licking at my lips.

"Help Kassidy!" Jude shouted to someone behind me.

Two hands appeared in front of my face, snatching Howard around his throat and ripping him from me. Doctor Fletcher slammed Howard into the wall again and again and again. I could hear his skull crack. Howard slumped, a path of blood dripped down the wall.

I tried to get up – my feet slipped. It was like being in an ice rink. The floor was coated in blood. My gown stuck to my skin. Doctor Fletcher pulled me up. His scrubs smeared in blood.

"I'm sorry, Kassidy," he whispered. "You need to get out of this place while you can – before the Cleaners turn up."

"Cleaners?" I panted.

"Not normal cleaners. You don't want to be here when they arrive," he said. "Now go."

"But…" I started.

"You go *now* before I change my mind," he snapped, his eyes darkening as he loomed over me. He ripped the tube from my arm. The bag of VA20 fell to the floor.

"*Leave!*" he shouted. His right arm sprang to the side, grabbing Wendy around her neck as she tried to snatch at me. He lifted her off her feet, flinging her like a ragdoll across the ward.

"C'mon, Kassidy!" Jude shouted. He was by the door, Raven stood behind him. Max took hold of my hand and pulled me along.

Reaching the door, I stopped.

"Where's Carly?" I asked. "We have to get her."

"No, we have to go," shouted Jude, holding me back. "I'm not going in there again. We need to find a way out of this place and fast."

"I'm not leaving without her!" I screamed. "She'll die in there."

"She's dead already," Jude shouted, pushing me out into the corridor. "I saw James pull her out from under the bed, Carly's gone."

He dragged me along the corridor. Max and Raven had already disappeared around the corner. Just as we reached the bend, they came running back.

"We can't get out that way," shouted Max. "It's locked."

"We'll have to go through Ward 1," said Jude, turning back.

"No way. I'm not going in there," hissed Raven. "It's evil, the devil works in there."

"Don't be so fucking stupid," said Jude. "The devil *isn't real*. Unless you want to take your chances with Ward 2 – I don't think we have any other options, do you?"

"I didn't think zombies were real until I spent a night of luxury on *Ward 2*!" I said, staring at Jude.

A noise came from around the bend in the corridor. Voices. Footsteps. Doctor Middleton and Doctor Wright. There were others, too.

We looked at each other. Panic spread across our faces.

"We'll have to go through Ward 1," I whispered.

We ran back. Jude and Max pulled at the rusty padlock barring our entry. I didn't know which way was best. Ward 2 was no good. Our escape through the corridor was now blocked; but what if Ward 1 was a dead end?

"Come on," I urged, looking at Jude and Max. They were kicking at the door. Panic raced through me as the voices down the corridor grew nearer. I flinched at the sudden thump against the doors to Ward 2. Something was trying to get out, I hoped it wasn't Simon or maybe Howard was still alive – trying to get out and finish me off.

"Done it, c'mon," said Max, the rusty padlock had given up the fight and now lay broken on the floor. Jude reached down and picked it up.

"We don't want to leave a trail of our escape for them to follow," he said.

Raven still hesitated. I grabbed her hand. If she didn't move now we'd get caught. Pulling her into Ward 1, Jude and Max shut the doors. I held my breath – afraid that Doctor Middleton would hear it. My heart thumped. Footsteps clattered past outside.

"Clean up everyone – *everything*," said Doctor Middleton from the other side of the door. "We can't have *anyone* leaving the building."

I looked round at the others. My eyes strained to see them through the dark. What the hell had just happened on Ward 2? What was *Cruor Pharma* up to?

CHAPTER EIGHT

"We need to stay quiet," said Jude. "I don't think they've noticed the missing padlock. Ward 2 looks like a bloodbath and it might take them a while before they notice that some of the volunteers are missing."

"Help me block the doors," I said, taking hold of a filing cabinet. "It won't stop them for long but it might give us a bit of time to run."

"Doctor Fletcher might tell them we've escaped," whispered Raven, flinching at the sudden sound of thunder from beyond the hospital walls.

"Fletcher must be dead," muttered Max. "There's no way he could've killed off all those *things* and live to tell the tale."

"I don't like it in here. Can't you feel it? Death lingers," murmured Raven.

"Shut up," spat Jude. "Someone will hear you."

Ward 1 lit up. The flash of lightning gave me a quick glimpse of my surroundings. Old hospital beds lay strewn across the floor. Blood-stained mattresses scattered the room. A struggle had taken place. A massacre. The windows had been boarded up. Tiny gaps between the planks allowed the lightning to burst through. I stepped forward. Catching my foot on something, I stumbled over. The sound clattered through the ward. We froze. Fearful that it would send the others looking for us.

"Are you okay?" whispered Jude, kneeling down next to me. "Have you hurt yourself?"

"I'm all right," I said, looking at what I'd fallen over. It was a drip. An empty bag still hung from it. Turning it over in my hands, I could just make out *VA10* written across the front of it.

"What is this stuff?" I asked. "Surely the people overseeing these trials must have known that it wasn't safe. Why let Cruor Pharma carry on with human testing?"

"Hey, look at this," whispered Raven, holding up a clear plastic bag.

It was full of large brown envelopes. There must have been at least twenty. Some of the contents had fallen out. Passports and mobiles lay at the bottom of the plastic bag. She pulled an envelope out.

"Those must be ours," said Max, grabbing the plastic bag from Raven.

"Robert O'Brien: VA10," Jude said, pulling an envelope out and reading the name on the front.

"Let me see." Max snatched it away from Jude.

"This one says, Sylvia Green: VA10," whispered Raven, tearing it open. She pulled out an iPod and a mobile. "We could call the police, tell them what's happened and where we are."

Jude grabbed the mobile from her hands. He pressed the button on the top and we held our breaths. Would it still have any life in it? How long had it been shut away on Ward 1?

"It's dead," he sighed. "It's been gathering dust for too long."

"Check the other envelopes. There must be more with phones in them. If mine's in there, it will work. I had plenty of battery life left," I said, grabbing the bag.

I tipped out the contents. Envelopes lay scattered around our feet. Max rummaged through them – reading out every name. When he'd got to the last one, he threw it down on the floor and kicked at the pile. Ours wasn't there. Every mobile was dead.

I sat down. My mind drifted back to Ward 2. Images of Howard crawling up my body – touching my skin, abruptly filled my head. His teeth biting my stomach, a bloody grin stretched across his face. I screwed my eyes shut. I could feel his hands slide over my chest – fingers tearing at my hair. His innards hot and wet – dragging over my skin. I shuddered.

"*Stop it*," I hissed to myself, brushing my gown down like I was knocking dust from an old rug.

"Hey, it's okay," soothed Jude, trying to hold my arms down by my side.

"I'm all right," I said, pulling my arms free. "I can still feel Howard touching me. I can smell him."

"He's gone", Jude whispered. "He's not touching you anymore. He's dead."

Jude put his arm around my shoulder. I felt my body calm as I took deep breaths.

"Kassidy, you'll be okay," he said, stroking the side of my face. "We'll get out of here and everything will be fine. *I promise.*"

"I'm sorry," I said, "I can't believe what I've seen here tonight – this just can't be real. Normal people turning into zombie-things and crawling along walls – what the fuck is going on?"

"I don't know," said Max, crouching down beside me. "But it's happened here before and we need to get out of this place."

"We'll probably end up twisted *like Raven* after this," whispered Jude.

"I'm not *twisted*," hissed Raven. "I just *sense* things."

The ward lit up again. Raven was standing in front of me. Her black makeup smeared around her face and her gown was speckled with blood. The crook of her arm was bruised. The veins running under her skin were swollen black. I looked down at my arm. It looked like Raven's. Was I going turn into one of those zombie things? Was she? I ran my finger over my vein. I cringed as I traced the lumps clotted up my arm. It felt tender.

"My arm looks like that," said Max, holding it out for me to see.

"Mine doesn't," said Jude. "It's just bruised where the needle went in."

"How come?" asked Raven. "Why hasn't it done the same to you?"

"How should I know?" he shrugged. "I'm not a doctor."

"Maybe you didn't get the VA20," said Max. "They do that sometimes in drug trials. What's it called? A placebo. I don't think May or Carly had it either, they seemed okay – no black veins up their arms."

"But why haven't we changed into those zombie-things?" I said. "I don't get it."

"Maybe we will," whispered Max. "I think we should all be honest with each other. If any of us starts feeling strange then we should say so. To protect each other."

"Agreed," said Jude, helping me up from the floor.

"Come on, let's see if there's a way out of Ward 1," suggested Max. "It's not gonna be long before Middleton and Wright come looking for us."

I picked up a passport and flicked through the pages. A photo of a girl – probably my age, stared out from the page. Her name was Sylvia Green. A consent form from *Cruor Pharma* was folded in the back. Was she dead? Did she change? Did someone kill her? Were any of these volunteers still alive? I took the passport and form with me.

We reached the end of the ward. A curtain was pulled across the back wall. I took a step forward and stood on something cold. I bent down, curling my fingers around an iPod. How did this get all the way down the end of the ward? Why wasn't it sealed in an envelope like all the other items had been? I tried to turn it on but, just like the mobiles, it was dead. I tucked it inside the passport. If I was gonna get out of here then at least I'd have something to show the police.

"There's a door behind the curtain," said Max, reaching for the handle.

"Wait, we can't just go strolling out," I whispered. "We need to check what's out there."

"I'll look," said Jude, taking hold of the door handle.

He pulled it open – just a fraction. We listened.

Silence.

He pushed his face to the gap – one eye peering out.

"What can you see?" I asked.

CHAPTER NINE

"It leads out into another corridor," whispered Jude. "I can't see much, it's too dark."

"Well we can't stay in here and we can't go back, so we may as well see where it takes us," I said, pulling the wet, clingy gown away from my skin. I was beginning to shiver – my skin damp with blood.

"Let's just get out of this ward, eyes are watching us," whispered Raven, looking over her shoulder at Ward 1.

"Of course there are, Raven," said Jude, rolling his eyes. "Are you sure you didn't pop some pills before you turned up here – Acid or something?"

"I'm not a *drug user*," spat Raven. "The dead *are* here, I can feel them! All those passports in there belong to the dead."

"So you're saying that everyone who has taken part in these *fucked-up* drug trials is *dead*?" said Max. His eyes had clouded over like a storm brewing in the sky.

"Yes," nodded Raven. "They're all dead."

"I refuse to believe that *any* company or person could get away with murder on such a large scale. When people go missing, relatives start asking questions – they go to the *police*," hissed Max, thumping his fist against the wall. "Some of those people *must* have escaped – they can't *all* be dead."

"Then why hasn't this place been shut down? Surely Doctor Middleton would be locked up by now," I whispered. "You only have to trace your steps back a short time. Ward 2 – *remember*?

"But we got out," said Max. "Those things didn't kill us – we're standing here now – *alive*."

"For how much longer? Yes, we escaped Ward 2 but we haven't escaped the building. We've got this far because Doctor Fletcher let us go," I said. "It won't be much longer before they realise they're a few bodies *too short*."

"I think we need to move on instead of standing here analysing," said Jude. "Let's just get the hell out and then we can think about what we are gonna do."

"There's no way we're going to get past the security guards dressed like this," I said. "There's loads of them outside."

"Don't worry about that now, let's just keep moving," whispered Jude, taking a step out into the corridor.

Raven followed close behind Jude – eager to be out of Ward 1. I stepped out next – Max trailed behind me. He seemed reluctant to leave the ward. Maybe fear was setting in? The unthinkable playing out in his head. That bag of passports and mobiles a frightening reminder that the other volunteers probably didn't make it out alive, making our chance of escape seem slim.

It was cold. Stone brickwork lined the walls. A barred window at the end of the corridor flashed with lightning, allowing us to see that whatever had gone on in Ward 1 had continued out in this corridor. Bloody handprints sprawled over the grey brickwork. I shuddered – footprints! The image of Simon scurrying along the walls in Ward 2 crept into my head. I looked up at the ceiling. Red footprints scattered along it. What the hell were those things? Once human but now…?

"Keep up," whispered Jude, looking over his shoulder at me.

I hadn't realised I'd stopped walking. Max was looking at the walls. He shook his head like he was unable to believe what he was seeing.

"What do you think happened to those things?" asked Max. "Do you think they're still alive? They must have got out of Ward 1 – the footprints go all the way down to the end of this corridor."

"I don't know," I shrugged. "But if they are alive, I just hope they're not loose and wandering around this building."

"Me too," he whispered. "Come on, we need to stay close to the others."

He placed his hand against the small of my back, guiding me toward Jude and Raven who were now at the end of the corridor.

"Which way should we go?" asked Raven, looking left then right. "There are doors down each corridor, we could check each room – see if there's a way out or maybe we might find a phone."

"There isn't going to be a phone in this part of the building," said Jude. "It's too old – you heard what Doctor Middleton said. This half of the building is only used now for overnight drug trials."

"We might find something else to wear other than these wet gowns," said Max. "I think we should look."

"We don't have time to go *window shopping*," hissed Jude. "We need to find a way out before they start looking for us."

A sudden noise coming from Ward 1 made us freeze. Metal scraping over tiles. I swallowed. The filing cabinet we'd put against the doors. My heart kick-started into heavy beats. My blood pulsed through my body too fast – jittering through my veins like flashing lights at a rave.

"*Quick,* in here," whispered Max, heading to the nearest door down the left corridor.

He grabbed the handle, twisting it to the right. It wouldn't open.

"Try the next door," said Jude, running past Max and taking hold of the handle.

It opened. We piled in – shoving our way through – desperate to hide from whomever it was coming through Ward 1. The room was dark with only one small window in it. A musty, mouldy smell filled the air.

"Find somewhere to hide," whispered Max. "Under the desk, two can get under there."

I ran round to the other side of the desk, catching a glimpse of myself in the long mirror fixed to the wall. What a mess I looked. I crawled in, still holding the passport and iPod tightly in my hand. Raven squeezed in after me. The floor was covered in filth – cobwebs stuck to my face. I could see Jude in the mirror. He opened a cupboard door – climbed in, pulling it shut. Max slipped under a bed – dragging some old blankets over the side to conceal himself. We waited. Those rave-type beats pounding in my ears – heart racing overtime.

"I'm scared," whispered Raven, eyes wide – a tear trickled slowly down her cheek.

"Shhh." I held my finger to my lips. "Just keep quiet. Whoever it is might not come in here."

The sound of a door trying to be opened cut into the silence. Footsteps coming nearer. They stopped. The creak of the door handle set my skin racing in goose-bumps. Light slowly seeped through as the door pushed open. Raven took my hand squeezing it tight. Peering at the mirror on the wall, I strained to see who it was. A key turned, locking the door. Heavy panting filled the room.

"Dear God, let me get out of here alive," murmured Nurse Jones, her ashen face appearing in the mirror. "Please don't let them get me!"

CHAPTER TEN

I didn't even consider if I should or could trust Nurse Jones before I climbed out from under the desk.

"Nurse Jones," I whispered. "It's me, Kassidy."

She jumped at my sudden appearance – shocked to learn that she wasn't alone.

"You're alive, I thought you must be dead," she said. "You need to get out of here. They're looking for me. They're going to kill me. I've seen *too* much."

"You've done these drug tests before, you must have known what they were going to do to us," I said. "How could you do it – you're meant to be a nurse – someone who cares for their patients?"

"No, I didn't know," she cried. "I've never stayed all night during a drug test. I'm working overtime. I usually set up the patients and then go home – *I promise*."

"What's in VA20?" Max climbed out from under the bed. "What happened to the other volunteers who had VA10 and VA00 put in them?"

"I don't know," she said, surprised to see him. "I thought they all just went home in the morning after the trials. I never saw them again."

"Did you see Robert O'Brien – was he one of your patients?" Max pushed. He held out a passport, the page opened on a photo of a blonde haired guy.

"I'm not… sure," Nurse Jones stammered. "Maybe – I can't remember."

"That's bullshit, she's lying," shouted Max, thumping his fist down on top of the desk.

"Keep your voice down, Max," hissed Jude, stepping out from the cupboard. "She obviously doesn't know any more than we do – do you?"

Jude turned Nurse Jones around to face him. He placed his hands on her shoulders and stared into her eyes.

"It's okay, I believe you," Jude said. "Max, leave the poor woman alone, she's scared half to death already."

"All I know about VA20 is…" she stopped. Low, moaning whispers echoed off the stone corridor outside the room. "They're coming for me."

"*Hide*," whispered Max pushing me toward the desk. He climbed back under the bed.

"If they find you, you keep quiet about us," said Jude, looking at Nurse Jones.

She pulled away from him, a look of fear in her eyes.

"I won't say anything," she whispered. "Where can I hide?"

"Get under the bed with Max," I said to Nurse Jones. "There's no room under the desk."

The door handle twisted. It creaked and groaned, unable to open from being locked. I huddled next to Raven, who sat with her eyes screwed shut – maybe she thought if she couldn't see anyone then they couldn't see her. I watched in the mirror as the door shook. I could hear breathing – rasping from outside. A loud thump hit the door. Then it went quiet – the door remained shut. I stared in disbelief as a shadowy mass seemed to come through the door, breaking into six forms. The shadows became solid. In one – two blinks of an eye, they had taken on the form of ghostly humans. Thick, black aprons were tied about them – plastic gloves all the way up to their armpits. Their lower faces were hidden behind black surgical masks – eyes dark and murky. They didn't speak – just rasped like their lungs were full of mucus and their leather aprons creaked when they moved. Were these the Cleaners that Doctor Fletcher had warned me about?

I held my breath – willing them to move on to another room. What would I do if they came around to this side of the desk? Could they see me in the mirror? I hugged my legs tighter to my chest, trying to be as small as possible.

A sob came from under the bed. Nurse Jones. Had they heard her? If they looked under there they would find Max, and if they found him then they would surely find the rest of us. One of the Cleaners slowly drifted toward the bed. I held my breath. The door was suddenly kicked open.

Doctor Middleton appeared in the mirror. He walked in and stood alongside the six Cleaners.

"Where is she?" he asked, his eyes wandered around the room.

The cleaner nearest the bed stretched his gloved hand down under the blankets – its arm extended at an unnatural length. It pulled Nurse Jones out by her ankle. She screamed.

"Please don't kill me, *please*!" she begged. "I won't tell anyone what I saw. Just let me leave and I promise you'll never see me again."

"I can't do that, Nurse Jones," Doctor Middleton frowned. "You need to be cleaned away."

Pulling out a chair, he sat down. "The cleaners will remove all traces of you," Doctor Middleton glared.

"I just want to *go home*," Nurse Jones screamed. "Why won't you let me go home?"

"You're no good to me now. If you hadn't stuck your nose in, then maybe I could have kept you, but..."

"My son will come looking for me, he'll go to the police and then they will come *here*," she cried. "*You won't get away with it.*"

Reaching out with his arm, Doctor Middleton snatched Nurse Jones around her throat. He lifted her up. Her legs dangled, swinging about like spaghetti. Nurse Jones' eyes bulged as Doctor Middleton pressed his fingers against her throat. She gripped his hand, trying to release the pressure around her neck. A gargled gasp escaped her lips as Doctor Middleton's fingers ruptured through her flesh. Blood surged down his arm – his fingers hidden inside her throat. His hand twisted left and right like he was turning a door handle. He dropped her.

I heaved. Hot vomit rushed up my throat. I swallowed it back down. It stung. With my hand clasped tight over my mouth, I fought to keep the contents of my stomach from exploding over the floor. I didn't want to end up like Nurse Jones. I looked at Raven. She still had her eyes shut – hands clutched tightly together against her chest, like she was praying.

"Clean her up, then go and find her son. Dispose of him. I don't want any traces left forgotten," said Doctor Middleton.

I looked at the mirror. The cleaners were bent over Nurse Jones' body. They tore off her arms. The wrenching and grinding of bones filled the room. They dismantled her like tent poles. I looked away. I didn't want to see any more.

"I've checked the bodies," came Doctor Wright's voice.

I looked back at the mirror. She stood in the doorway still in scrubs – not one drop of blood down them, although the same couldn't be said for her face. Blood was smeared around her chin and on her nose like she'd been punched and got a nosebleed.

"Has everyone been accounted for?" asked Doctor Middleton, turning toward a small sink by the door. He turned the tap and washed his hands clean of blood.

"There seems to be three missing," she said. "They must be somewhere in this part of the building."

"Have you told the security guards outside? We don't want them letting the volunteers escape," he asked, drying his hands on a dirty old towel.

"I've told them to not let anyone out unless they have their I.D. badge," Doctor Wright answered. "They haven't forgotten what happened on the last drug trial. Most of them are too scared to mess up."

"Do we have any idea what state the volunteers are in? Have they changed like the others?" asked Doctor Middleton.

"I think if they had changed like the others then we would know about it – don't you think? We'd hear them turning on each other. There would be trails of blood and body parts everywhere," said Doctor Wright.

Rubbing his hands together and a glimmer in his eyes, Doctor Middleton said, "Good, this could be it. This could be what we've been waiting for. We need to find them quickly and get them locked up. I don't want them escaping into the country, never to be seen again."

Doctor Wright smiled. "Is that all?"

"No. Has there been any sighting of my son yet? I'd like to know what he's playing at," asked Doctor Middleton. "He should have been helping on Ward 2, not doing a disappearing act."

"I asked Doctor Fletcher but he said he hadn't seen him. As for the volunteers escaping, I think Doctor Fletcher needs talking to," she said. "How did they get past him?"

"You leave Fletcher to me, it's not your place to question him!" snapped Doctor Middleton.

She nodded her head and stepped out of the room. The cleaners had filled several black sacks with Nurse Jones' body parts. As the sacks were lifted up, a steady stream of blood splattered onto the floor.

I held my breath. Had they finished in here? I watched as the cleaners drifted from the room like mist swirling over the ground. Doctor Middleton hung back. A look of concern etched across his face. Was he thinking about Doctor Fletcher – wondering if he had helped us escape?

He started to pace up and down, mumbling to himself. He stopped and bent down. When he stood up again his hand was covered in Nurse Jones' blood. It dripped from his skin as he inspected his fingers. He jerked forward like someone had pushed him from behind. Standing on the spot, he swayed back and forth – a dumb expression on his face – eyes rolled back in their sockets – mouth hanging open. His arms dropped down by his sides. He stayed like that for what seemed like an eternity as if in some kind of a trance, and then all of a sudden his body jerked back into life. He choked and gagged like there was something stuck in his throat. Straightening himself up as if he was checking that his limbs were working, he walked out of the room.

    The door shut. The room fell silent.

CHAPTER ELEVEN

Jude came out of hiding first. He tiptoed to the door – ear pressed against it – listening. Max slipped out from under the bed avoiding the blood puddled on the floor.

"Did you see what they did to Nurse Jones? They pulled her apart – bit by bit," I whispered, crawling out from under the desk. "They're freaking crazy, *insane*! What are they? They're not human – they just appeared in the room without opening the door."

"Like ghosts you mean?" asked Raven.

"I don't know, but they're not like us," I said, chewing on my fingernail.

"Ghosts can't hurt you," whispered Jude, "ghosts aren't real."

"Yes they are, I can feel them," hissed Raven. "This place is full of the dead."

"I thought Nurse Jones was one of them. I should have helped her – stopped them from taking her," said Max, shaking his head.

"You would've ended up dead as well," said Jude, running his hands through his hair.

"I wish I hadn't listened to *you*. You said there was nothing to worry about. Drug trials were safe – I had nothing to fear," hissed Raven, pointing a finger at Jude.

"Hey, drug trials are safe. I've done them before. How was I to know that this place was nothing but a slaughterhouse run by fucked-up *mad people?!*" spat Jude.

"Enough," I snapped. "I wasn't sure about doing this trial but at the end of the day it was me who decided to go through with it. Jude didn't force me – no one did. It doesn't matter now, Raven, we did it, and we can't take it back. We've got to find a way out of this place – that's what we should be doing, not blaming each other."

"Kassidy's right," whispered Max. "Now's not the time to turn on each other. That might happen later when this *shit* flowing through our veins works its way around us, but for now, while we're all sane, let's just find a way out of here alive."

I looked down at my arm. The black lumpy fluid had travelled further up my vein and spread out looking like a tree branch.

I walked over to the mirror. My blonde hair was now matted with blood – May's blood. I shut my eyes, willing the image of her falling toward me – throat ripped open by Wendy, away. I shuddered.

A hole in my gown reminded me of Howard's snapping jaws as he bit through the fabric puncturing my flesh. My stomach felt sore.

I needed to check it – clean it up, or it would get infected. I almost laughed. *Infected*. My whole body was probably infected by VA20 and I was worrying about a *bite mark*. I took a closer look at my face. Dried blood stained my skin. I was covered in it. It was like I'd had a bucket of red paint thrown over me and it had all run down over my body. My face was coated in May's hideous death and it had dried into long, red streaks.

Reaching behind I untied the top string of my gown and pulled the fabric down over my shoulders. A thin black line just under the skin had journeyed its way up the side of my neck. What would happen when the drug reached my heart? I didn't know what to think anymore. My head hurt. I was tired. I looked like I had crawled out from a car crash. Why had I ignored the warnings inside my head – the anxiety I had felt standing in line waiting outside? Why hadn't I just got a job? I hadn't sold my body for sex but I'd sold it to Cruor Pharma. I looked away in shame. Why had I been so stupid? There really was no turning back. I'd made my bed and now I had to lie in it.

The sound of running water stirred me from my thoughts. Raven was scrubbing her face – wiping away the smeared black makeup from under her eyes. She wasn't as bloodied up as me but she held the same traumatic gaze in her eyes.

"Does anyone know the time?" I asked, looking toward the small barred window. It was still dark. The night seemed to drift on endlessly. I wanted daylight. For some reason the thought of a new day made everything better – like waking from a nightmare. Only I knew deep down that this nightmarish ordeal was going to follow me everywhere I went. No daylight was gonna help me.

"I don't know the time," said Jude, "but I reckon it must be the early hours of the morning. Maybe 3 a.m.?"

"Another couple of hours and it will be light. If we can get out of here, we should head down Strangers Hill toward Holly Tree and go straight to the police," said Max, pulling his hair back from off his face. His ponytail had long since fallen out and his shoulder length hair now hung in blonde-bloodied strands. He still held the passport in his hand.

"The police won't help us," said Jude. "What do you think they'll do when they see the state of us? Pat us on the head and say *'there,there'?!*"

"Of course they will help us – they have to," said Max, "it's their job."

"They'll lock us up and throw away the key," snapped Jude, running his hands under the tap and splashing water across his face.

"Why would they do that?" said Raven. "We've done nothing wrong."

"Look at your veins," said Jude, grabbing Raven's arm. "You'll end up in another place like this. Tested on, needles stuck in you, and if you turn into one of those creatures like Howard or Wendy, then you'll never see the light of day again."

I looked down at the floor. Jude was right. We'd be nothing more than dangerous freaks – unsafe. Too risky to be let loose with the public. But what if they *could* find a cure? Surely someone out there could help us, a scientist or a doctor. But could I ever trust another doctor again? Would I really want to go back into a hospital after having spent such a fucked-up night in Cruor Pharma? Maybe I wouldn't give a shit – maybe when I'd changed into one of those freaky zombie things, I'd be more than happy ripping large chunks of flesh from people. Nah – I couldn't live like that. I had never hurt anyone before and I didn't want to start now. There had to be something that could get this drug out of me. I couldn't give up hope yet.

"So what do you think we should do then if we get out of this place?" I asked. "Where will we go?"

"We'll hide out somewhere and then take it from there," said Jude. "I have a place where we could go, but it's in Wales. If we can get to my car we could use that to travel up there."

"Where's your car?" asked Max.

"I left it outside a bar in Holly Tree. I was too pissed to drive it home the other night," smiled Jude. "It's by The Fallen Star – you know it?"

"I've been there," I said. "It's full of piss-heads. Buy one get one free on a Friday night. Me and my friend Hannah go there sometimes."

"Look, I'll go down to Holly Tree with you, but I'm not going to Wales," said Max. "I'm going to the police. This place needs shutting down and those doctors and cleaners need locking up."

"Max, those cleaners can't be locked up. They evaporate through doors – I saw them," I said. "They're not human."

"I have to go, Kassidy – I need to find my brother," Max said. "This is his." He held up the passport.

So Max wasn't really here to save enough money to buy his own place. He had come looking for his brother. Why hadn't he said anything before? Not to draw attention to himself perhaps. To slip past Doctor Middleton and the others so he could have a nose about? I could understand that.

"Robert's been missing since he came to this place about three months ago. I've been to the police but they said it was just a missing person's enquiry and nothing more. The police said he would probably turn up at some point. I told them that he had gone to Cruor Pharma for a drug trial and all they said was that he'd probably gone off abroad to some place nice with the money. The police checked his bank account and the money from Cruor Pharma had been deposited into his account and taken out the day after his drug trial. They said that Cruor Pharma was a respectable company – did plenty for the local community and would never get mixed up in anything criminal. But I have his passport now and its proof that Robert hasn't left the country. That's why I came here, to look for him. When I saw the advertisement in the paper from Cruor Pharma, I knew I had to volunteer."

I looked at Robert's passport photo. He was blonde like Max – a bit older. Looking at Max, I could see the pain in his eyes. He needed to know what had happened to his brother. He needed to find out if Robert was still alive. But after everything I had seen in this place, I didn't think Max would have a happy ending. His brother was probably dead. I thought about the passport and iPod I had taken from Ward 1. It was under the desk still, where I'd hidden earlier. If I took them to the police with Max then maybe they'd listen more seriously to us.

"I'll come with you," I said.

"What? Are you two mad? Haven't you listened to a word I've said?" snapped Jude. "They'll lock you up and then come looking for me and Raven."

"We don't have to tell them about either of you," I said. "What about you, Raven? What do you want to do?"

"Leave me alone," she hissed. She fell to her knees clutching her stomach. Her eyes had gone a cloudy red. "It *hurts*," she mumbled.

"Shit, she's changing." Max backed away, grabbing my arm, pulling me back.

Jude bent down next to Raven. He looked into her eyes. "She's not changing, not like Howard or the others did. It's different." He looked up at Max and me.

"Raven, do you think you can walk?" I asked. "If we can find a way out then maybe we can get you some help."

"She'll slow us down," said Jude, standing up.

"Please don't leave me here – *please*," she whispered. "I don't want to die."

"We're not gonna leave you, you're coming with us," I said. "Max, help me get her up."

He hesitated.

"When this shit starts happening to me, I don't want to be left behind – I'm sure neither of you two want to be abandoned either," I glared.

"Kassidy's right, we can't just walk away and leave her," said Jude. "Take my hand and I'll pull you up, Raven."

She gripped his hand. Jude steadied her as she stumbled forward, her arm clutching her stomach. Raven's greasy black hair hung over her face – red, hazy eyes peered out from beneath it. She looked sickly.

"Okay, which way should we head?" I asked, splashing my face with water, trying to scrub the blood away. "There must be a staircase leading down to the ground floor somewhere."

"Let's go left when we get out of this room and see where the corridor takes us," said Jude. "And remember to stay quiet."

"We still need to find some clothes and I.D. if we're gonna walk past the security guards," whispered Max. "You heard what Doctor Wright said – we won't ever get out of here without them."

I walked over to the desk. Bending down, I fumbled around, grabbing the passport and iPod. The thought of going back out into the corridor scared the shit out of me, but what other choice was there? Raven needed help and it probably wouldn't be much longer before I needed help, too. If we could just get out of Cruor Pharma then maybe we could think more clearly. Maybe someone out there would help us.

CHAPTER TWELVE

We followed Jude. None of us spoke. The only sound I could hear was the patter of rain against the windows along the corridor. The thunder and lightning had stopped. I was relieved to see no bloody handprints or footprints at this end of the corridor. Max seemed more at ease with Raven. He helped her along, asking every couple of minutes if she felt okay. I kept checking over my shoulder, making sure that no one was creeping up on us. I hated being at the back – I felt vulnerable, but then I didn't want to be at the front either – not knowing what was around each corner. I didn't know what to fear more – the cleaners, the zombie-things, or the doctors.

"I've found the stairs," whispered Jude, looking over his shoulder at us. "Let's just look over the top and see if it's clear to go down."

I gripped the wooden banister and slowly lent over. The stairwell was dark but I could just make out the bottom. The floor was covered in crap. Rubbish lay discarded – broken glass, newspapers, and a hospital trolley turned on its side.

"Looks safe to go down," whispered Max. "But we'd better be careful not to knock any of that mess over or we'll make too much noise."

"Let's go then," said Jude. "But watch your feet, there's broken glass everywhere and we don't have shoes on. He lifted his foot and wriggled his toes as if to prove the point.

Taking hold of Raven's arm, I helped her down – glad to be in the middle of our group and not at the back.

"How are you feeling, Raven?" I asked. "Does your stomach still hurt?"

"The pain has eased," she whispered, "but look." She held up her right hand. The fingernails had grown. They looked more like claws – sharp and slightly curled over at the top. Half of the nail was covered in black polish but the new growth was a cloudy grey. Black veins pulsed across the top of her hand and around her wrist.

I looked down at my own fingernails. They still looked normal – half chewed, but *normal*.

"Do you think we'll get out of here?" asked Raven. "I just want to go home."

"I don't know," I said, shaking my head. "I still feel like I'm in a bad dream – like it can't be happening – like I've stepped out of reality and into hell."

Jude had stopped at the bottom of the stairs. There were two doors, each with a small, glass panel. One led into another corridor and the other – outside.

Max tiptoed across the cluttered floor, avoiding the shards of broken glass. He grabbed the door handle, twisting it gently.

Locked.

"Can you see anyone outside?" I asked, stepping over the mess.

"Stay away from the window," whispered Jude. "If security are out there they'll see you."

I stepped back, my foot catching on an old newspaper. I was about to kick it away when a picture on the front caught my eye. I crouched down and lifted up the yellowing paper. Trying to straighten the dog-eared pages, I noticed the date – 18th November 1974. My eyes widened as I looked at the picture. Doctor Middleton stood inside a shiny clean laboratory, microscope in front of him. A small article was written underneath.

Doctor Middleton – leading scientist in DNA research opens new building at Cruor Pharma.

With many successful findings from researching DNA and knowledge in aspects of human biology, Cruor Pharma has seen their profits and revenues increase.

"Identifying new links between diseases or the way in which people respond to treatments is key to increasing our chances of developing effective drugs," Doctor Middleton was reported to have said. "The new building will help us to examine further clinical data, run more tests and study DNA changes in genes."

Cruor Pharma is a privately run company situated outside the town of Holly Tree, Essex, and is a respected establishment among the local residents, running many charities and giving back to the local community. A new library and two police vehicles are just a couple of examples of the company's generosity. With sixty percent of the town's population working for Cruor Pharma, it isn't too hard to see why this company is so popular in Holly Tree.

I threw the paper down. It wasn't difficult to see how Doctor Middleton had covered up what he was really doing here. Even back then in the seventies, he had the locals eating out of his hands. No wonder poor Max didn't get anywhere with the police regarding his missing brother. I looked down at Sylvia Green's passport still clutched in my hand. This had to go some way in showing the police that all was not well at Cruor Pharma. Maybe the iPod I'd picked up would hold some kind of evidence too.

"Listen, everyone," said Jude. "We're not gonna get out through that door so we'll have to go down this corridor and see if there's another way. Be careful – make sure you keep away from the windows."

Pushing open the door, we followed Jude down the corridor. I wished I had another set of eyes in the back of my head. I was constantly checking over my shoulder at the barred windows and the ceiling for any signs of more bloody handprints. My ears were on constant alert. I flinched at every little noise and gasped at shadows flickering through the windows onto the brick walls.

As we came to the end of the corridor, it opened up into a large room with four doors. Rusty chairs lay scattered about the filthy floor. Old posters hung in shreds from the walls, and thick cobwebs dangled down from the broken light bulbs.

"This looks like some kind of waiting room," I whispered, walking over to a door. A small plaque was fixed to it. "Doctor Langstone," I read. He was the guy who was meant to be running the drug test but had been taken ill – or at least that's what that old cow, Doctor Wright had said to me.

I twisted the door handle and opened it up just a little, enough for me to make sure that it was safe to go inside. The room smelt stale, but I stepped in. It was empty. Closing the door, I walked over to Max and Jude. Raven was sitting on one of the rusty chairs, her red eyes staring at blankly ahead.

"That room is empty," said Max, pointing toward a door. "Let's hope there's a way out through one of the other two, otherwise we'll have to go back the way we came."

"Well, that one says treatment room and there's no sign on the other one," whispered Jude. "I think we should try the door with no sign."

He clambered over the chairs, his hospital gown catching on the rusty metal legs.

"Come on, Raven," said Max. "You don't want to stay here by yourself."

She stood up and struggled her way through the fallen chairs. Her hospital gown flapped open at the back, revealing a faint black vein snaking down the length of her right leg.

I looked down at my feet – my legs – they were clear. I breathed a sigh of relief. I still had time to get out of here and get help – stop this drug from consuming me.

"I'm not going down there," hissed Raven. She had stopped just inside the doorway of the unmarked room. "There's something bad –

festering evil – let's go back the way we came, *please*."

"Don't start with that shit again," said Jude. "The only thing that's festering is *you*. We don't have time to go back – we need to get out."

I looked at Raven. I didn't know if she really felt these things or whether it was just paranoia – but who could blame her, after everything that had happened – was *still* happening? I stared into the dark passageway and could see a set of steps. They disappeared down into a gloomy hole. I looked back at Raven. I could feel the same fear that she felt. Alarm bells were ringing inside my head, just like the ones I had heard when I was waiting in line with the other volunteers yesterday… and look what had happened when I ignored those warnings.

"I think Raven's right," I whispered, "this whole place is bad, but down there feels freaking worse. I don't like it."

"We *can't* go back," spat Jude, "we've been lucky getting this far without anyone spotting us. We must be near to an exit. If we go back the way we came you can be sure we'll get caught."

"Let's just go down the steps and see what it's like," whispered Max. "It can't be any worse than what we've already been through."

"I don't want to go through what I've already been through – *again, thanks, Max*," I said. "I'm not ready to die – I don't have suicidal feelings and I don't want to be taken apart by those freaking cleaners. I think we should head back."

"Look, let's not start losing the plot now. We need to stay calm. We need to stay together. We're not gonna get out of here if we split up," said Jude. "If those cleaners come back then we'll fight them or we'll hide."

"*Fight them* – are you out of your freaking mind, Jude?" I said. "You didn't see what they did to Nurse Jones – how they took her apart – how they came through the door. You were hiding in the cupboard for fuck's sake. No one is gonna fight those cleaners and come away smiling. I don't know what they are, but they aren't human."

"Okay, okay," whispered Max. "Let's have some peace. Fighting amongst ourselves isn't going to help. I know you're both scared but we have to go down those stairs. Going back is never a good idea. Jude, you can go first, then you, Kassidy. Raven, I'll stay behind you."

I looked at Raven. Her hands were clasped tightly together. Her red cloudy eyes wet – a tear trickled down her cheek. I pushed my fingers through my knotted bloody hair and let out a sigh. Closing my eyes, I shook my head. I wanted to wake up. I wanted this to be over. But every time I opened my eyes I was still in the same shit. Why wasn't there a solution, why couldn't I get out of this mess?

CHAPTER THIRTEEN

The stone steps were cold against my bare feet. I was sure the temperature was dropping with every step I took, down into the dark. My blood-stained gown had dried into a stiff clump of material – creased and irritating my skin. It did little to keep the chill air from nipping at my body.

Jude had taken my hand in his – guiding me down the stairs as it grew darker. If I hadn't have felt so worried about coming down here, I probably would've slapped his hand away, still feeling pissed off with him for being so flippant about fighting the cleaners. Max too, had wound me up.

The stairs led down into a narrow hall. Cracked tiles lined the floor and the stone brick walls had crumbled, leaving a breadcrumb-like dust all over the floor. The sound of dripping water echoed from down the hall.

"Please can we go back?" whispered Raven. "This is a bad idea."

"I know it is," I said, still gripping tightly to the passport and iPod I had taken earlier. "But we're down here now so let's just keep going."

We followed the hall round to the left. The atmosphere almost seemed to change from scary

to freaking menacing. It was like something
looming over us, shrouding us, swallowing us up.
Something waiting – expecting us. Raven's freaky
outbursts didn't seem so freaky now. The sense
of evil was almost overpowering. There was
something festering down here. Building up
strength. I slowed. My feet didn't want to go any
further.

"Can you feel it?" I whispered to Jude.
"There's something down here. I don't know
what it is, but..."

I stopped. A door at the end of the hall
with a glass panel almost seemed to bulge in its
frame. Icy cold swirls of air floated around it like
fog rolling over the ground. The hallway seemed
to close in, trapping us, squeezing us – not
wanting to let us go.

"Keep moving," whispered Jude. "The hall
bends round to the right. We don't need to go
into that room. Just go past it. Whatever is inside,
don't let it distract you."

I turned round and looked at Max and
Raven. After everything we had seen, this was
the first time I had noticed Max look scared. He
had taken hold of Raven, his arms tight around
her waist – looking over her shoulder. Raven's
hands grasped Max. Her eyes wide – mouth open.

I tiptoed. The nearer I got to the door, the
louder my heart thumped. A low moan

murmured from the room. Was it the Cleaners or those zombie-things from Ward 2? I forced myself on. Each step warning me to go back. My eyes never leaving the glass panel in the door – scared that something would suddenly appear – a face – a monster.

"Don't stop," whispered Jude, pulling on my hand. "Ignore the door. You don't want to see what's in there. None of us do."

I hadn't realised I'd stopped, the glass panel just inches from my face. My heart ticked like a bomb about to go off. I stepped nearer. A force almost willing me to look raced through my body. I slammed my fists against both sides of the door. Something pushed me. My nose touched the glass panel – my eyes adjusted to the view inside the room. A table and two chairs were placed in the middle of it. A candle flickered, creating dancing shadows across the walls. I turned to Jude, who was trying to pull me away.

"I can't see anyone in there – its empty," I whispered.

"Come away from there," said Jude. "It's not safe."

I looked back at the glass panel. This time my view was blocked. I gasped – momentarily stunned. A face stared out at me. One hand clawed at the glass panel – nails scraping down – screeching. I pulled away.

"Oh, my God, it's Carly," I whispered. "I thought you said she was gone – dead?"

"*Help me!*" she screamed. "Get me out of here."

"Take these." I shoved the passport and iPod into Raven's hands.

I grabbed the door handle. Pushing and pulling. It wouldn't budge. Carly's frightened eyes stared out at me.

"Help me open the door," I said, looking at Jude and Max. "We've got to get her out."

"Leave her," warned Jude. "She's not right." He tried to pull me away from the door.

"I'm not leaving her again," I shouted. "She's just like us. She hasn't turned into one of those things."

Carly started to bang on the door. "Please don't leave me, *please*." She stepped back. The door suddenly flew open. I felt myself sucked in. The door slammed shut. I turned, grabbing the handle – twisting it – yanking it – kicking it. I was trapped. I spun around. Carly was standing by the table.

"Carly, we need to get out of here, help me open the door!" I shouted. I turned back. Max was at the glass panel. He was tugging at the handle – the door rattled.

"Mmmmm. Mmmmm," Carly now hummed. Her shoulders were hunched over – blonde hair draped across her face – eyes peering out at me. She swayed on her feet – backwards – forwards.

I stepped back, inching slowly toward the door – my eyes never leaving Carly. Her arms were covered in black veins. They twisted under her skin like long bendy sticks of liquorice. Her toenails had gone a cloudy grey-black and were warped out of shape. She continued to watch me – humming – swaying.

From the other side of the door I could hear Raven crying out, Max yanking on the handle, and Jude shouting.

Carly took a step toward me. Lifting her face, she grinned. Her teeth had gone black – congealed blood stuck between them. She laughed – jellied clots of blood spraying over the floor. A deep, low cackle seemed to come from within, like it wasn't really her. I froze. I didn't know what to do. I looked around the room, searching for something that I could use against her. The chairs? But I would have to get past her to reach them. Fuck that – I wasn't going anywhere near her. I stood with my back against the door.

"Max, get the *fucking* door open!" I shouted, my hand blindly felt for the handle. I found it – wrenched it down. It did nothing.

"Bitch, *fucking bitch!*" screamed Carly, her voice was deep – male. She let out another laugh, low – guttural.

I gasped in air. My body shook. Feet glued to the floor – frozen like a statue. I had nowhere to run. Nowhere to hide. Tears welled up in my eyes. Lips quivering, I waited. Unsure – like a frightened animal caught in the beams of a car's headlights. What was her next move?

"Try talking to her – calm her down," shouted Jude, shoulder-barging the door.

"*What*? Talk to her? I don't think talking is gonna help, Jude," I snapped. I wasn't on some freaking T.V. talk show.

"Talk to me, *bitch*," a throaty male voice came from Carly.

"Listen to me, Carly, it's me, Kassidy." My voice trembled. "You remember me, don't you? I'm your friend."

"You *fucking* left me – you *filthy whore!*" screamed Carly, her body started to fit – shake – convulse. A rage emanated from within her. The table flew across the room smashing into the wall – splintering over the floor. Carly's body lifted – threw itself up – smacking into the ceiling. It hurled itself across the room – hitting the wall and plummeting to the floor. She stood up. Stretched – bones crunching. She hobbled toward me – grinning.

The room had turned icy-cold. I could see my breath swirling in front of me. I shivered. The candle lay on the floor – still lit. If that went out then I would be blind to Carly. I shuffled to my right – back still tight to the wall.

"Please, Carly, don't hurt me – *please*." I held my hands up in front of me – the only barrier I had.

"Your dad was a *fucking dick*," spat Carly, vomit dripping from her mouth. "He's in *hell*, he can't hear you when you speak to him at his grave. He *hates* you – every time he had to look at you it made him reach for the next bottle of whisky. He tried to drown you out by drinking. You let him down – you never made him proud – you were a drain on his life. You're nothing but a *fucking waster* – he never wanted you – you sent him *to hell*."

I shook my head, backing away from her as she came nearer. How did she know my dad was a drunk?

"Your mother loathed you – that's why she dumped you – that's why she's dead. She wanted you dead – *bitch*," hissed Carly, her voice deep and gruff. "No one wants you – no one loves you – you're gonna *burn* in hell."

I nearly toppled over as my foot stepped onto the broken leg from the table. I snatched down – gripping it in my fingers. I swung it – smacking it over Carly's head. It cracked in half. Carly snarled. Snatching a clump of my hair, she pulled me to my knees and jumped on my back. My head smacked against the floor. Again and again. I couldn't get her off. Her strength was too much – *unnatural*.

"I'm gonna fuck with you! Kassidy," Carly screamed, clawing at my face. "Fuck you, fuck you – *fuck you*." She pulled at my gown – her fingernails slicing into my back.

With all my strength, I flung myself over to the right, knocking Carly from off me. She leapt from the floor – throwing herself on top of me – pinning me down – her face inches from mine. Her breath stank. It filled my nostrils - the smell of rotting meat. It was unbearable. It was suffocating.

"*Get off of me*, please, Carly," I screamed, bringing my knee up and wedging my foot against her stomach. Her face leered at me – it seemed to distort – twist screw-up on itself – like something inside her was trying to break out.

"I'm not fucking Carly, you *stupid bitch*," she hissed. "Carly's dead. I've taken her – I'm gonna take you, too." She bit down into my neck.

I screamed. I kicked out at her – lifted my other leg and wedged it against her stomach like I'd done with the other one. I pushed with my feet, using them like a lever. I couldn't shift her. Her teeth still clung onto my flesh – stretching – tearing the skin as I tried to lift her away from me. I grabbed a handful of Carly's hair, and she released her bite. I pulled her head up so she was facing me. Curling my fist, I punched her in the face. She didn't flinch. A deep, menacing laugh seeped out from Carly's mouth.

"You like playing?" Carly's throaty voice spat. She threw herself up to the ceiling, taking me with her. I hung in the air – my legs kicking wildly about. Carly's hands held me up by my neck. I couldn't breathe. I panicked. I tried to loosen her grip on me. Just when I thought I was going to pass out, she flung me across the room. My body crashed into the wall. I slid down it, dropping to the floor.

Stunned, I lay there watching Carly. She crawled toward me, like a tiger hunting its prey. My eyes moved over to the door. It had gone quiet out there – no sign of Jude, Max, or Raven. Had they left me like we'd left Carly?

As if reading my mind, Carly knelt over me and said, "They don't give a shit about a filthy *fucking pussy* like you. You're nothing but a *pissing whore.*"

The room went dark. The candle had gone out. The only light now was coming through the small panel of glass set into the door. But it offered little light. I couldn't see Carly. She was no longer leaning over me. The room had fallen into silence. I pushed myself up into a sitting position. My body hurt – my head thumped. Where was she? I looked back at the door. I could make a run for it but what would be the point? It probably still wouldn't open. I shifted sideways on my arse – little shuffles at a time – nearer and nearer to the door. My eyes were on constant alert for any movement within the room. It was like a game of Hide and Seek, only with deadly consequences if I was found.

"You're gonna die, Kassidy, *fucking die*! Go to hell, *bitch*," Carly suddenly screamed from the darkness. A chair came hurtling toward me. It smashed down over my head by unseen hands.

I crawled across the room, kneeling up at the door – stretching – trying to reach the handle – one last chance to escape. As my hands curled around it, I was yanked back by my ankles. I slid across the floor. Carly stood laughing. She started to fit again. She scraped her fingernails down her face like she was trying to shed her skin. Deep scratch marks appeared down her cheeks. Her body was thrown against the wall, head smashing repeatedly against it. It was like there was someone behind her, forcing her into the wall. She screamed, only this time she sounded like Carly.

"Help me, Kassidy! He's inside me, I can't get him out," she cried.

"I don't know what to do, I don't know how to help you?" I panicked. Should I go over to her? Help her? Hold her down and stop whatever it was smashing her head into the wall? I couldn't just stand and watch her body break – watch Carly die. Cautiously, I stepped toward her. Fear speeding through me – rushing at my heart – making it jump – skip – jump. I reached out for her. Carly stopped. She stood still – facing the wall.

"I think it's gone," she whispered.

She turned round. Her face bloodied. Her eyes crazed. A malevolent grin spread across her face.

"Dumb bitch," she spat, her voice male – gruff again.

I turned – fled across the room toward the door. It flew open, almost knocking me over. An arm reached through the gap– fingers grabbing the neck of my gown. My feet left the floor. Doctor Fletcher pulled me out and the door slammed shut behind me.

CHAPTER FOURTEEN

I stood in the hall. Doctor Fletcher loomed over me. His blue eyes looked me up and down like he was deciding what to do. I couldn't speak – my breathing too fast – too deep. My lungs ached. I slumped down – elbows resting on my knees – head in my hands. Carly's room silent now, like it was empty.

"Did it hurt you?" asked Doctor Fletcher, crouching down beside me.

I looked at him. "What do you think? Look at me. I'm covered in bruises, scratches, and if that's not enough, take a look at the *fucking bite mark* on my neck," I snapped. "I've had my hair ripped out and my veins filled with black *shit*. Yeah – I think I'm fucking hurt – *don't you*?"

Doctor Fletcher took hold of my arm. He ran his fingers slowly up and down the black lumpy veins.

"How far has it spread?" he asked, looking at my legs.

"I don't know?" I shrugged. "I haven't had a chance to strip off and admire the new look I've gained."

His hand reached down – fingers lightly against the inside of my thigh – pushing up the stiff fabric of my hospital gown.

I slapped his hand away. "I don't think so – you're not looking up there," I glared.

His eyes sparkled. Was that a grin I could see him trying to hide? Better not be.

"Where are the others?" Doctor Fletcher asked, taking my hands and pulling me up.

I looked down the hall. "I don't know – they disappeared when I got trapped inside that room. They tried to open the door but it was locked."

I looked over at the glass panel. It was clear. No Carly peering out at me this time. I shuddered. The atmosphere was still charged with something evil – something waiting to jump out at me.

"We need to get you out of here, Kassidy," said Doctor Fletcher. "The Cleaners are looking for you and the others."

"What are the Cleaners? I saw them take Nurse Jones apart," I whispered. "They aren't human. Doctor Middleton isn't human and neither is that thing in there." I pointed at the door. "It can't get out of there, can it?"

"No, it's trapped inside the room. But you're not safe. There are others – some like Carly, others different – wandering around this hospital," he whispered. "You have to get away before they find you."

A deep, husky laugh came from Carly's room. I stared at the glass panel, expecting to see her face leering out at me. It was empty. The laugh came again, sending shivers through me.

"Come back in here, Kassidy," hissed a male voice. "Let me fuck you – *fuck you in hell – bitch.*"

I gasped. I took a step closer to Doctor Fletcher.

"It can't get you, the door is locked," he said.

"Locked doors don't seem to mean much in this place," I whispered. "They open and shut and suck you in – those Cleaners managed to find a way through a locked door."

Doctor Fletcher looked at his watch. "Listen, the night shift will be leaving in a couple of hours. That's going to be the best time for you to get out of here. There'll be loads of staff leaving and the day shift will be turning up – plenty of people to hide amongst. All you need is a uniform and an I.D. badge," he said, looking at my hospital gown. "You'll never get past the security guards on the gate looking like that."

"Can't I just climb over the wall and make a run for it? I don't want to go past the security guards – what if they don't recognise me as one of the staff?" I asked.

"Like I said, the gates will be busy. Security won't be paying too much attention. You could try climbing over the wall if you can avoid the security cameras and barbed wire, but I really don't fancy your chances of succeeding, Kassidy," said Doctor Fletcher. "This place is built to keep people out and volunteers in."

"The dumb bitch is gonna *die* – she's gonna rot in hell." Carly's face suddenly appeared – claws tapping slowly on the glass panel. She let out a raspy laugh – vomit exploding from her mouth, hitting the glass and running down in thick, black, mushy lumps. Her skin hung from her face where she had ripped and clawed at it.

"Come on, I know where you can hide out for a while – where you'll be safe." Doctor Fletcher took my hand and gently pulled me along the hall.

I stopped – yanking my hand from his. What was wrong with me? Why was I trusting a guy who had played a part in setting me up – choking my veins with a drug that was probably gonna kill me? For all I knew, he could be leading me back to Doctor Middleton and the Cleaners. Why did he care now? A little voice inside my head answered my questions – *you have to trust him, he's all you have. He knows what's happening to you – he's gonna help you escape. He's the one with all the answers. You don't have any other choice.*

"We don't have time to hang about, Kassidy," said Doctor Fletcher, taking hold of my hand again. "If you want to get out of here, then you need to come with me."

"What about Max, Raven, and Jude?" I asked. "I need to find them."

"Why do you care about them? You don't really know them." Doctor Fletcher lent over me – his blue eyes searching – challenging me.

"I can't just leave them here," I whispered, taking a step back from Doctor Fletcher's stare.

"Why?" he asked, stepping nearer to me – closing the gap between us.

His stare flustered me. I took another step back, banging into the crumbling wall – sending small lumps of brick tumbling to the floor.

"I don't want to be the only one out there like this." I held my hands up. The black veins had spread to both arms now – weaving under my skin like straws filled with blackcurrant juice. "I don't want to be alone. If I start changing into one of those zombie things like Wendy and Howard did, then at least I'd have Jude and the others with me – they might be able to help me. Stop me from hurting people – stop me from eating people."

"You think someone like Jude is gonna help you? Guys like him won't help you – he'll just lead you into trouble." Doctor Fletcher lent over me, resting his hands against the wall – closing me in – lips just inches from my neck. "Don't trust him."

"I trusted you up on Ward 2," I whispered. "You said there was nothing to worry about. You said you wouldn't hurt me." I looked into his eyes. His gaze seemed to swallow me up – drown me – *charm* me. "I trusted you and looked what happened."

Doctor Fletcher placed his hands on my waist. He pulled me toward him.

"You know you can always trust a doctor." His eyes glimmered. "Now, do you want my help or not?"

CHAPTER FIFTEEN

Doctor Fletcher walked quickly down the hall, pulling me along behind him. I struggled to keep up – limbs stiff and bruised.

Apart from the drips of water echoing along the hall and the sound of our footsteps treading over the clutter thrown about the floor, it was silent. There was very little light, but Doctor Fletcher seemed to know these corridors and hallways like the back of his hand. To me it felt like I was going round and round in circles – trapped in a maze – every corridor like the last one.

I had so many questions I wanted to ask. I needed answers, but would Doctor Fletcher tell me anything? He'd pretty much blanked any questions I had asked so far. Maybe if I tried to get to know a bit about him – tell him a bit about myself – he would be more willing to give up some answers.

"What's your name?" I asked, trying to keep up beside him.

He turned his head – eyes narrowed – like he was wondering why I had asked.

"I have many names, Kassidy. But you can call me Ben Fletcher," he said, stopping outside a door and pulling a key from his pocket. He pushed it into the lock, turning it to the right. It clicked open. I followed him through. He shut the door behind us and locked it again. My eyes adjusted to the dark and I could see I was in some kind of treatment room. An examination bed was placed in the centre. There was a trolley beside it with rusty surgical instruments covered in dust and webs. Tatty cabinets hung from the walls, some lopsided. The smell of damp mixed with dust and dirt blocked my nose, making me choke.

"How long have you worked for Cruor Pharma? I coughed, trying to cover my nose and mouth with my hand, hoping it would stop the dust irritating the back of my throat.

"Years – not as long as Doctor Middleton and Doctor Langstone though," he answered, walking toward a door at the back of the room.

"Doctor Langstone is the one in charge here, isn't he?" I said, tucking my hair behind my ear.

"On paper he is, but Doctor Middleton runs this place now. Doctor Langstone decided to move back to the other site, Cruor Pharma's sister company. He didn't like Doctor Middleton's way of running the company. He never comes down here now – stays up north working on blood samples," he said, taking out another key and unlocking the door.

I wasn't surprised at all to hear that Doctor Langstone didn't like the way things were done here. This place was fucked up. It sounded to me like Doctor Langstone had done a runner – wish I had done the same.

"Ben." I held my breath, wondering how he'd react to me calling him by his first name.

He turned and looked at me – expression blank. His blue eyes – crystal like gems. "What is it?" he asked.

"Am I going to end up like Carly? Or like Howard and Wendy?" I screwed my hands tight into fists – scared of hearing his answer but needing to know.

"I don't think you will be like Howard or Wendy," Ben whispered. "I think if you were going to end up like them it would have already happened." He locked the door behind me. "Come on, we need to keep moving."

I walked beside him. A part of me relieved that I probably wouldn't turn into some zombie-thing, but Ben hadn't said I wouldn't turn out like Carly.

"What is VA20? What is it doing to me?" I grasped his arm, a sudden panic flared up within me – thoughts of Carly – insane – deranged threw my heartbeat off balance.

He pulled his arm away from my grip and continued to walk toward a staircase at the end of the hall.

I grabbed his arm again – stopping him dead in his tracks. I was angry. I had a right to know, I wasn't going to let him blank me anymore. He turned slowly toward me. His clear blue eyes dark now – stormy.

"What is VA20? I need to know – *am I gonna die*?" I snapped, frustration rising through my body. "You stuck this *shit* in me – the least you can do is tell me what the fuck it is and if you've given me a death sentence."

Ben curled his hand around my throat – slamming me into the wall. His sudden attack took me by surprise. His eyes stretched wide – pupils black – like two smouldering pots of tar. A dark shadow almost seemed to fall upon me. My hair fluttered across my face as a cold gust of air swept past. I tried to push him away – hands hitting his chest – he didn't move – he was solid – unbreakable.

"*I don't have to tell you anything!*" he shouted, his face in mine. "*Don't push me, Kassidy.*" He released his grip on my throat, turning away from me. He paced up and down the corridor – deep breaths – in-out. He held his head in his hands – like he was suffering a migraine. I watched as he mumbled to himself.

He kicked out at an overturned metal cabinet. The noise clattered down the corridor – echoing up the staircase. I held my breath, fearful that the noise would send the Cleaners our way. I listened. My heart thumped. I took a breath – relaxed a little. I couldn't hear anyone coming. I looked at Ben. He seemed calmer. He had stopped pacing and mumbling to himself. He stood with his back to me. Should I approach him or just stay where I was? Ben turned slowly and grinned at me. A shiver ran down my spine. A look of evil etched across his face.

"Come here, Kassidy," he hushed, holding out his hand. "I'm sorry I shouted at you, I didn't mean to hurt you."

I gulped hard – swallowing down my fear. Maybe if I went to him he would calm down – go back to how he had been. I needed his help. What would be the point in running? Where would I run to? I forced my feet to move. He beckoned me over – lips smiling. He opened his arms – pulled me to him. I felt his body press hard against me. His strong arms wrapped tight – hands sliding lower down my back.

"Look at me, Kassidy," he whispered, his breath hot against my neck. "You are easy to manipulate – I love that."

I looked up. The whites of his eyes cloudy-black as if staring into my soul. His body felt hot

– like a fever burning through my hospital gown. He pushed his face into my hair – breathing in my scent – a look of ecstasy in his eyes. He lowered his face – lips brushing mine – sending a hot flush over my skin. I gasped – but I didn't move – didn't pull away. He was soaking me up – swamping me – tempting my body to give into him. His touch captivated me – held me still – kept me in a trance. I didn't want him to stop. I felt his hands slide up beneath my gown. I was burning from the inside. His fingers stroking my arse – his lips pressed hard against mine – tongue breaking through – washing the inside of my mouth. He pushed me up against the wall – his leg sliding in between mine.

"Am I tempting you, Kassidy? Do you want me to take your body?" Ben whispered, his hands mauling me – nails clawing down my back – his touch burning through my skin.

"Yes," I breathed, running my hands up his chest under his scrubs. His body was firm – my hands almost seemed to smoulder at the feel of his skin. I was on fire – ablaze – so hot I thought I would turn to ash. I shut my eyes and melted against him.

"Kassidy, what are you doing?" Ben asked, holding his hand up against my forehead. "You've been standing with your back pressed up to the wall, mumbling to yourself. Are you feeling ill?"

"What?" I gasped opening my eyes. "You were kissing me... you had your hands up..." I stopped. I could feel my face flush. Ben stared at me.

"I didn't kiss you," he said. "You feel really hot, you must have been hallucinating."

"No, I wasn't. You were touching me, *I felt you*," I argued. "I didn't imagine it – I'm not *freaking crazy*."

"Look, we don't have time for this. I need to get you to the south side of the building. There's a door hidden from view of anyone walking past outside. It's covered by a huge oak tree," Ben said, walking up the stairs. "I have the key. When you get outside, you need to turn left and follow the path until you come across some steps leading down a small slope. When you get to the bottom, turn right and follow the path until you get to the chapel."

"Then what?" I asked, still feeling confused. I was sure Ben had kissed me – touched me – how could I conjure up something so vivid – so intense? My skin still felt his scorching touch. But how had it all started? What had we been doing before he'd begun *assaulting* me? I just couldn't remember. Maybe he was telling the truth? Maybe I was going crazy? But he did touch me up on Ward 2 – didn't he?

"Are you even listening to me, Kassidy?" Ben had stopped halfway up the stairs – hands on his hips – a look of frustration across his face.

"Huh? Yes I'm listening," I said, catching up to him. I hadn't heard half of what he'd said to me. Just something about a key and a chapel. I couldn't concentrate. I looked at my gown – checking to see if it had been ruffled up – if it was still in place. Nothing seemed disturbed – the gown was still tied tight at the back. I felt stupid. It had been so real – now I was second-guessing myself – doubting my sanity.

"Take the key now – I have to leave you before we get to the door." He handed me an old rusty key and carried on up the stairs.

"Aren't you coming with me?" I asked. The thought of having to wander through the rest of this hospital alone didn't do much for my nerves, and even though I wasn't sure if I could trust Ben, I still would rather have him with me. I wished Jude and the others would show up – maybe they had already got out.

"I can't go with you. They'll wonder where I am soon and come looking for me – if you're still with me then they'll never let you leave," whispered Ben, turning down a corridor lined with barred windows. "You're their miracle breakthrough, Kassidy – if they get their hands on you then you'll never see the light again."

"I guess there's no point in asking you what kind of a miracle breakthrough I am – you won't tell me – will you?" I whispered, checking over my shoulder – making sure we were alone.

Silence. That was my answer. Ben continued down the corridor, stopping outside some double doors. There was a sign swinging from a hook which read *Canteen*.

"This is where I say goodbye." He turned to face me. "You need to go through the canteen and the kitchen. There's a door that leads out into a hallway. Turn left. Don't take the door on the right. When you get to the end of the hall you'll see the old fire exit – remember to head for the chapel – wait inside until the night shift changes over."

"What about my clothes? Where am I gonna find a uniform?" I asked.

"There must be an old one lying about somewhere," he said. "You could try searching the lockers in the staff room – it's next to the kitchen."

I nodded my head. After everything I had seen in this place – everything that had happened to me – you would think I couldn't wait to escape, but going outside, back into the real world scared the shit out of me. What was I going to do? What was going to happen to me?

How would I cover up these black veins twisting around my body?

"Kassidy, be careful when you get out. Don't trust anyone. There are so many people living in Holly Tree who work here. No one is safe to trust," he whispered, taking hold of my hand.

"What should I do?" I asked, the feel of his hand comforted me – made me feel safe.

"That's up to you," he said. "I'm sorry I can't help you anymore. If you want answers you could try finding Doctor Langstone. He might help you or he might not. Cruor Pharma's sister company is based in Monsal Head, Derbyshire, but Doctor Middleton still has contact with some of the scientists up there. You can't just go strolling in. You need to be careful."

"Why have you helped me?" I asked, staring into his eyes, hoping he would answer me.

"If Doctor Middleton gets hold of you, he'll ruin you," Ben whispered. "You didn't end up like Wendy or Howard and you might think that's good, and it is in a way, but if you end up like Carly you'll be lost forever – tortured. I helped you because I know how it feels to live a life of suffering – living like a puppet – your life is no longer your own – your movements, your voice, all controlled by unseen puppet strings."

Ben turned away, lost in his thoughts. I had no idea what he was going on about. Too much had happened to even think straight. My head felt ready to crack open – full to bursting – exhaustion clutching at my body – dragging me down – pulling on my limbs. My eyes burnt – lids heavy.

"Maybe it's too late to help me," I whispered, glancing down at the black veins. "Maybe you should have helped me sooner – like not sticking that freaking needle into me." I walked over to a window and grasped the iron bars. The sky was calm now, no more rain fell and the wind had dropped. The storm had moved on – soon the night would do the same.

"It's not too late for you, Kassidy, you just need to get away from here," Ben said, turning me around to face him. "I'm sorry I did this to you, I can't control myself sometimes. You have no idea what it's like to be manipulated – dominated against your will."

Ben's eyes clouded over again. He stared deeply – like he was trying to see behind my eyes – into my soul. I stepped away – unsure of him – his strange mood swings made me wary – he was unpredictable.

"If you're really sorry, then tell me what VA20 is," I said, hoping the question wouldn't enrage him again.

"It's a real mixture of things – I can't tell you," he sniggered. That look of evil darkening his face again – a menacing presence shadowing over me.

"What are you?" I whispered, looking over my shoulder – seeking an escape.

"I'm evil…" He laughed. Ben shook his head like he was trying to rid himself of something. "I'm not safe to be around, Kassidy. Go now before I can't stop myself."

I looked at the canteen door then back at Ben. Was he really going to let me go? His eyes had cleared again – that crystal-blue gaze lingered over me. He smiled but this time it was genuine, not evil. I stepped toward the canteen door – my outstretched arm hesitating.

"Why don't you come with me, get away from here – find help?" I asked. There was something about Ben that made me want to help him, something hidden deep beneath his tanned skin and crystal-blue eyes. There was another part of me that wanted him to go with me for my own selfish reasons – he was after all the only person who had the answers to what was happening inside of me – the only one who had done something to help me. I knew I shouldn't trust him, but I wanted to.

"Be careful what you say to me. *Don't* invite me to go anywhere with you – I might just latch on to you and then you'll regret it," hissed Ben. "There is no helping me, and if they get their hands on you – if *I* get my hands on you – then you'll be the one screaming for help. Now get the *fuck* out of my sight before I take you."

"Okay, I'm going," I whispered. My hands pushed open the canteen doors, I turned to look back one last time at Ben, but he'd already gone.

CHAPTER SIXTEEN

The canteen doors swung shut. I found myself inside a large hall. The high ceiling was lined with broken windows – vines hung from shards of glass like thick lengths of rope. Dripping water splashed onto the old rotting lino-covered floor. I hugged my arms tight around me, waiting for my eyes to adjust to the dim surroundings. There were five long rows of tables that stretched all the way down to the end of the hall. Chairs were pushed in under them – some kicked over amongst the rubble. I walked slowly down between the tables, my feet scattering broken plates and cutlery – echoing through the room. I gripped the key that Ben had given to me. It gave me hope – my escape out of this hell-hole. My thoughts returned to Ben. He was one big mystery – a puzzle. But then again, my feelings toward him were nothing but a mystery. I should hate him – loathe him for what he'd done to me, but I didn't. I should be scared of him but I wasn't – well, maybe a little. I was confused. This place had really messed with my head. A bird squawking above me made me jump. I fell sideways into one of the tables sending its rotten cutlery sprawling over the edge, falling to the floor. The sound of breaking plates and metal jugs hitting the ground echoed around the room causing more birds to flutter about above me.

"Shit," I cursed under my breath. With all that noise I wouldn't be surprised to see Doctor Middleton or the Cleaners appear. I stood still – straining my ears – waiting to hear footsteps coming. Nothing. Just the sound of dripping water and wings flapping. I tiptoed on through the mess – little jumps over piles of clutter and filth like I was jumping on stepping stones. There was a gap in one of the rows of tables and I squeezed through. An old vending machine up against the wall caught my eye. I looked through the glass panel. It still had chocolate bars and crisps stocked in it – packets of Treets and Spangles, KP Discos, and Space Raiders. My stomach rumbled. I needed food. I needed sleep. I caught sight of my reflection in the glass panel. Dried blood stained the side of my neck where Carly had bitten me. My face looked a mess – my eyes smeared black with mascara. My appearance made me think of Carly. What had they done to her? She had looked like Carly but she acted like someone else – like someone had taken her over. The things she had said about my dad crushed me. How had she known such personal things about him? And my mum – was it true what Carly had said? All I knew about my mum was that she had died when I was two years old. My dad had never wanted to talk about my mum. I didn't even know where she was buried. I had never even seen one photo of her. I carried on through the hall, pushing thoughts of my dad and mum from my mind. Old posters and photos fluttered against the walls – a cold breeze drifted down from the broken windows above me. I looked back toward the canteen doors. I had made it halfway through the hall. Where was the door that led into the kitchen? On the other side of the room I could see a large hatch. It was shut. My eyes drifted along the wall until they reached a door right at the end of the room – the kitchen. Clambering over some chairs, I headed across the hall. I stopped. Something made me hesitate. A feeling – a sense that something was coming. I wasn't going to ignore those inner feelings anymore. I had made that mistake too many times already. Getting onto my hands and knees, I crawled under a table. I waited – my heart beating fast. The atmosphere darkened. I looked toward the canteen doors then back at my escape route through the door into the kitchen. It was too far to get to without being seen by whatever was coming. I could feel myself trembling. What was I going have to face this time? The Cleaners? Doctor Middleton? Carly? Ben had said there were others like Carly wandering around this place – I didn't know what was worse. I screwed my eyes shut, willing whatever it was to pass by the canteen and leave me alone. I opened one eye and looked at the canteen doors.

"Please don't come in here," I whispered. "Please don't find me."

The doors wavered slightly. I swallowed back a gasp threatening to erupt from my throat. A cold, menacing breeze filled the hall. Dark shadowy shapes seemed to push through the canteen doors. I knew at once what they were – the Cleaners. They stood still – listening, watching, waiting for a noise or movement. The silence filled me with dread. I knew I had to keep perfectly still. One tiny movement would create so much noise with all the cutlery and plates all over the floor. My left knee was resting on top of a fork, and if I moved they would hear it. I had managed to stay hidden from them earlier so maybe if I just kept still they would move on to the next room. Their shadowy shapes had taken on a more solid form now and I could see their long, plastic aprons and gloves. Their faces were still hidden behind black surgical masks. They moved forwards slowly – the creak of their aprons echoing around the hall. They stopped at the first row of tables. One of them suddenly crouched down and peered under. Another cleaner drifted over to the second row and got down on his hands and knees and crawled under, pushing his way through the chairs and clutter. The scraping of metal filled the hall and sent birds flapping and squawking around the broken windows in the ceiling. I was under the fourth row of tables. I looked to my left. There was only one more row between me and the door to the kitchen. But even if I managed to get under the last line of tables I would still have to break cover and make a run for the door. I was only halfway down the hall, and although it wasn't much of a distance to reach the door, it was still too far a gap to outrun the Cleaners. I faced front. A cleaner had moved over to the third row. The tables in front of him suddenly lifted up by unseen hands and were thrown across the hall smashing into the walls. I flinched at the deafening noise, panic rushing through me like a tidal wave. Tears welled up in my eyes. Was this it? Was this my end? My row of tables was next. My body shook with fear as I saw two boots appear ahead of me. Any minute now and the cleaner would be looking under or throwing the tables aside. I wanted to run. I wanted to scream. But fear kept me rooted firmly under the tables. Just as I expected to see the cleaner's masked face peering at me, its boots lifted up and disappeared. I swallowed back my tears. It was walking along the tables. I could hear its footsteps coming nearer. The tables groaned and shook. I couldn't see it but I knew the cleaner was only a short distance away. I gasped as I saw its long gloved arm swiping around – seeking me out – stretching under the table. The arm disappeared again. I looked up through the tiny gap between the table I was crouched under and the table in front of me. I waited – breath held tight like I was underwater. The table in front wobbled. A dark shadow fell over the gap. The cleaner was almost over me. I felt myself sway – still trying to balance on all fours – knee still resting on the fork. The hall had fallen silent. Did they know I was under here? Were they trying to sweat me out – see if I made a run for it? A black gloved hand suddenly snatched down beside me – grasping at air. I leant over to my left, trying to avoid its grip. Its creaking fingers clenching – searching – just inches from my face. The hand swiped about like it was trying to catch a fly. It caught hold of my hair and yanked some strands out, almost pulling me off balance. I watched as the hand disappeared above me, blonde wisps of my hair still caught in its grasp. The cleaner knew I was under here – he must know. He would have felt the tug of hair caught between his fingers as it yanked the strands free from my scalp. I waited, my body tense. Short, sharp breaths escaping my lips. The wait was agony. What was his next move? As if in answer, blonde wisps of my hair floated down from above the table, landing beside me amongst the dirt and clutter on the floor. I looked to my left – searching for the easiest route toward the kitchen door. I couldn't go under the fifth row of tables, there was too much blocking my way. I would just get caught up among the broken chairs and rubbish. I would have to go over the fifth row and run for my life. Should I go now? Should I wait and see which direction the cleaner would attack from? Looking forwards I could see five sets of boots standing at the end of the row I was hiding under. It was like a game of cat and mouse. I screamed as the cleaner's face suddenly appeared to my left. It was leaning over from the top of the table – face upside down – raspy breaths seeping through its mask. Its eyes were black – intimidating. Its shadowy form not quiet solid, almost like a cloudy, transparent black mass. It stretched out its arm snapping at my wrist. I grabbed a broken chair leg and smashed it down over the cleaner's arm. It seemed to fall through its body like I had thrown it through thin air. I scampered out from under the table – key gripped tight in my hand and hurled myself across the last row of tables scattering plates and cups with me. I landed on my feet and ran for the kitchen door. I didn't look back. I was too scared. Splinters of broken glass stabbed at my feet as I ran across the hall – tripping and sliding over the mess. Reaching the door I grabbed for the handle. Yanking it down I prayed that it wasn't locked. It opened. As I turned to slam the door shut behind me, I saw the Cleaners walking toward me. I pulled the door shut, and spotting a bolt at the top I slid it across. I knew that wouldn't stop them from getting in but it might give me a few seconds start to find somewhere to hide. I backed away from the door, knowing that their shadowy forms would soon start to filter through. Turning around I found myself standing between stainless steel kitchen worktops. Saucepans and cooking utensils hung from hooks covered in thick cobwebs. I ran through the kitchen looking for somewhere to hide. There were only small cupboards with doors hanging off them and a large freezer which wouldn't open. I looked back at the door half expecting to see the Cleaners appearing, but it was clear. As I raced through the kitchen I noticed fresh footprints clearly marked on the dirty tiles. They went in the direction of the door at the far end of the kitchen. Whomever they belonged to had been through here recently. I stopped in the middle of the room – hesitating – not sure if I should hide or go the way the footprints went. I didn't want to run into anyone else. That dark, menacing feeling seemed to be creeping into the kitchen and I looked over at the bolted door. Relieved that I couldn't see the Cleaners, I turned away but something caught my eye. The hatch that I had noticed in the canteen seemed to be darkening. The Cleaners were coming through. A dark, hazy cloud started to form into six shapes. I panicked. Grabbing hold of a large, dusty ladle and knife, I held them up in front of me, ready to hit out. The ladle slipped to the right, falling over the knife – forming what looked like a cross. The Cleaners' dark shapes shuddered and shrank, disappearing back through the hatch. What did I do? Dropping the knife and ladle, I turned and raced past the kitchen worktops and threw open the door into a hallway. I went left – remembering Ben's directions, but stopped abruptly when I heard whispering voices at the end of the hall. In a panic, I turned around and ran the other way. The hallway curved round to the right and then split into two directions. A large, heavy door swayed on creaky hinges. I pushed through it. I needed to get out of the hallway before the Cleaners came back. There seemed little point in running deeper into the hospital only to get lost by myself, and besides, I was so close now to the door which Ben had directed me to – the door which would get me out of this hell-hole.

CHAPTER SEVENTEEN

With my heart still racing, I stood with my ear up against the door, listening. My body trembled with adrenaline and I breathed in deeply, trying to fill my lungs with air. There was no noise coming from the other side of the door, and the whispering voices seemed to have disappeared. Waiting another few minutes, just to make sure the Cleaners weren't coming, I turned to face the room. I was standing in a small office. It was filthy, just like the rest of the building. Yellowed paperwork lay scattered all over the floor and on top of a desk. Rusty old filing cabinets lined the stained walls and an old-fashioned typewriter with some of its keys missing was covered in thick cobwebs. A metal door at the end of the room with a large handle seemed to be the only thing not covered in dirt and grime. The office had a strange smell about it. It wasn't the usual smell of damp and dust, it was something more repugnant – sickly. It made my stomach churn. The small barred window at the rear of the room allowed a little light to seep in – the dark night sky had turned to a grey swirly mist – not quite morning, but not night either. Leaning against the wall I let myself slide down until I was sitting on the floor. My heartbeat had calmed a little and I sat staring into space, my mind blank – the horrors of what I had seen here refusing to compute. I tried not to think about what had happened. I didn't want those images of Carly, May, and Wendy entering my mind. Ward 2 popped into my head and I screwed my eyes shut – willing it to go away.

"Think of something nice," I whispered, straining my memory for happy times, but no matter how hard I tried, all I could see was death in the most repulsive ways. I looked down at the rusty key still gripped tightly in my hand. I would wait another ten minutes before attempting to reach the door to the outside – just to be sure that the hallway was clear of Cleaners and the whispering voices. I picked up some of the yellowed paperwork scattered about me. The writing had long since faded away. I dropped it back on the floor and stood up. I walked over to the desk, knocking a half burned candle over. Placing the key down and pulling open the drawers, I hoped to find something that could help me get past the security guards at the gate. An I.D. badge would be good, but I wasn't that lucky. The drawers contained nothing more than pens, matches, and paperwork. As I closed the drawer, my eyes fell upon the metal door at the end of the room. I cautiously stepped toward it, gripping the large handle. Maybe I would find something in there. A box of old latex gloves were fixed to the wall beside the door. Pressing my ear to the cold metal, I listened. There was no sound coming from the other side. I yanked down hard on the handle and pushed the door open. The smell hit me like a slap to the face and I gagged. Covering my nose and mouth with my hand, I peered into the room. There was barely any light and I strained to see what was inside. The floor felt cold against my bare feet. I pushed the door fully open and stepped in. I fumbled around for a light switch but couldn't find one. Probably wouldn't work anyway, I thought. I walked back into the office and removed the matches from the desk drawer. Picking up the candle and standing it up on the desk I lit a match. The candle flickered a small, warm glow and I carried it back through the metal door. The light wasn't enough for me to see the back half of the room so I slowly tiptoed in. Holding the candle up in one hand and covering my nose with the other, I noticed a small sink in the corner of the room. It looked more like a toilet being so short and low down to the ground. The floor and walls were tiled and lined with metal cabinets. Taking my hand away from my nose I pulled one open and found what looked like surgical instruments scattered over the shelves – knives, scissors, and large tweezers all rusted and worn. This must have been some kind of treatment room or operating theatre, I thought. Checking back over my shoulder to make sure I was still alone, I continued through the room. Hanging from a hook were some aprons and I fumbled through them, hoping I might find something else to wear other than this blood-stained hospital gown I had on. My heart leapt with excitement as I came across a black jacket tucked behind the aprons. Placing the candle on the floor, I pulled the jacket from off the hook. I could wear this over the gown. At least it would cover up the dried blood and might just look like I was wearing a dress under the jacket. Not everyone left work in their uniforms. All I needed now was a pair of shoes and some I.D. I pulled the jacket on. It was a little big but I didn't care. I felt glad to have another layer of clothing on – less vulnerable. As I bent down to pick up the candle, I froze. The flickering light illuminated a fresh, wet, red smear across the floor tiles heading toward the back of the room. The realisation that someone had been in here recently sent chills through me. I stood up slowly. Holding the candle out in front of me, my eyes followed the red smear until it stopped and turned into more of a congealed puddle under a long metal tray on wheels. It was pushed up against the back wall. A blood-soaked sheet lay covering something on top of it. Then noticing the back wall, I took in a sharp breath. It was lined with small metal doors. Some were open with trays hanging out. I was in a morgue. Looking back down at the blood-soaked sheet my heart thumped uncontrollably. The sheet twitched. I backed away. My foot slipped in the wet smear and I toppled over, dropping the candle. A deep moan from the back of the room sent fear racing through me. Snatching up the candle I tried to get back on my feet. A hand shot out from under the sheet frantically grabbing with its fingers. It snatched at its cover and pulled the bloodied material from off its face.

"Wendy," I gasped, the smell from her rotting body making me gag.

Her face looked bloated – skin hung from her cheeks like rotten stringy beef pushed through a mincer. Thick, black veins twisted up around her neck. She stretched open her mouth – gums oozing a thick grey mush – teeth gone. A high-pitched wail came from deep within her as she sat up on the tray. Using her left hand she pushed the tray away from the wall – it rolled toward me on its squeaky wheels. The sheet fell to the floor. Her black, rotting legs were covered in huge, slushy blisters that seemed to bubble and pop, releasing a bloodied puree. I kicked out at the tray, sending it hurtling back into the wall.

The force sent Wendy rolling off the side and she hit the floor. Her flesh splattered over the tiles. It was like meat falling from the bone. A loud rattling sound echoed through the room as one of the small metal doors that lined the wall started to shake. Something was trying to get out. Wendy grabbed at the tray as she tried to stand up but her legs just seemed to be melting into like slush. She fell back down, a raspy cackle escaping her lips – eyes staring wildly at me.

"I want you," she spat, grey, lumpy phlegm spraying from her mouth.

She used her body to roll toward me, turning easily across the floor in all the blood and flesh. I spun around and raced for the door – slipping and skidding as I went. Grabbing onto the metal handle, I slammed the door shut with all my strength. I had to get out of here. I didn't want to be anywhere near Wendy and whatever else it was in the morgue. Snatching up the rusty key, I headed for the office door which led out into the corridor. Before I'd reached it, the door burst open.

"Shit, you scared me. I thought we'd never see you again," Max said, coming toward me, a wooden chair leg in his hand.

I opened my arms and hugged him. Never had I been so pleased to see someone. I held him tight not wanting to let him go – afraid I might lose him again.

"We need to get out of this room, Max," I breathed, looking into his eyes. The door to the morgue suddenly rattled.

"Who's in there?" he asked, holding up the chair leg ready to strike.

"It's Wendy. Or what's left of her," I said, pulling Max toward the office door.

CHAPTER EIGHTEEN

We slipped out into the corridor. Max held my hand tightly and led me toward another door.

"Where are the others?" I asked, hoping I would see Raven and Jude again. "Are they okay?"

"They're fine. We've been hiding out in the locker room trying to keep away from the Cleaners," he whispered, pushing open a door.

Stepping in, I saw what looked like a changing room filled with several rows of battered lockers, a small cupboard up against the far wall, and some metal poles lying among the rubbish scattered over the floor. Raven sat on a wooden bench. She was trying to push her foot into a black boot. She looked up, surprised to see me.

"Kassidy! Oh, my God, I thought you were dead," she said.

"You think everyone's dead." Jude stepped out from behind a row of grey lockers. He grinned at me and held out his hand for me to take. "Where the hell did you disappear to? We went back to that room where Carly was but you'd gone – vanished. Raven thought Carly had eaten you."

"No I didn't," she hissed, standing up, hands on her hips. "I thought that Carly had killed you."

"Well, where had you three gone?" I asked. "You left me in that room, I thought I was gonna die."

"We tried to get the door open but it wouldn't budge. And then we heard someone coming and we ran," said Max, leaning the chair leg up against the lockers. "When we went back to that room the door was still shut but you weren't in there, just Carly."

"Doctor Fletcher got me out," I said, sitting down on one of the benches. I was still feeling shaky after seeing Wendy.

"Fletcher?" whispered Max. "Why did *he* help you? He's one of the bad guys – it doesn't make sense."

Jude tutted and shook his head, a look of disapproval etched across his face. "You can't trust that guy, he's messing with you, Kassidy. He probably let you out because it's all part of his sick, *fucked-up* game. Where is he now?"

"I don't know. He left me outside the canteen, gave me this key, and told me which door to go to," I said, holding it up. "He said to wait in the chapel until the nightshift swaps with the dayshift. The gates will be busy then and we might be able to slip out unnoticed amongst the staff."

"What chapel?" asked Raven, squeezing her other foot into a boot.

"It's in the grounds of Cruor Pharma, but Doctor Fletcher said we'd be safe there," I answered, slipping the rusty key into the jacket pocket I was now wearing.

"Yeah and Fletcher said VA20 was safe," huffed Jude. "I'm not going to that chapel, it's just some kind of trap."

"What would be the point in him trapping us at the chapel? Why let me go when he could have just kept me? He could have easily handed me over to Doctor Middleton," I said, standing up and walking over toward a row of lockers.

"Look, I don't trust any of these doctors but what Kassidy says makes sense. He wouldn't let her go just so he could catch her again. We all heard Middleton and Wright talking in that room where Nurse Jones got killed," said Max. "They don't want us escaping out of the hospital, that's why the Cleaners are looking for us."

Raven stood up. She had found a pair of what looked like porter's trousers and a jacket to match. It was the perfect fit. She tucked her hospital gown into the trousers and pulled the jacket tight about her. All she needed was an I.D. badge and she was good to go.

"I'll go to the chapel," she said. "It's got to be better than hanging around in here being chased by the dead."

Jude rolled his eyes. "Why stay at Cruor Pharma when we could just climb over the walls and make a run for it? Going to the chapel is just delaying our escape."

"We'll never get over those walls without being seen by the cameras or security guards," said Max, pulling on a grubby pair of old jeans. "And anyway, have you seen how tall those walls are? We'd need a ladder."

"The chapel is a bad idea," said Jude, turning away and rummaging through a locker for something to wear.

"I think it's the best option we have," I said. "The door to the outside isn't far from here, we could be out of this place and in the grounds within five minutes."

"We know where the door is," said Raven. "We tried to get out of it a little while ago but it was locked, and then we heard someone running about down the corridor so we ran in here and hid."

"So does everyone agree that we head for the chapel and try and walk out with the rest of the staff?" asked Max. He had pulled off his hospital gown and was now slipping on a black leather jacket that had been left inside one of the lockers. His right arm had one black vein snaking around under his skin. The VA20 in him hadn't spread as far as mine and Raven's had. Max pulled up the zip of the jacket and brushed the dust off from the shoulders, sending dust motes swirling about the room.

"Yes, I agree," I said, looking for a pair of shoes.

"Me too," said Raven, her black greasy hair hung over her eyes like slimy lengths of seaweed.

"I don't have much choice, I guess," muttered Jude. He reached round and untied the strings at the back of his gown. It dropped to the floor and he stood in his boxer shorts. His skin was perfectly smooth – no ugly black veins marked his body. Raven peered out from under her black fringe at him. Her eyes soaked up every part of his body. She saw me looking at her and turned away, embarrassed that I'd caught her eyeing Jude up. I couldn't blame her. He had a body that any girl would want to feel against their skin. It was faultless – picture-perfect.

After opening several lockers and finding them empty I came across one that had a pair of black shoes. They were scuffed at the toes and smelt musty but I didn't care. Anything would do. I tried them on. They were a little too big and slipped off my heels as I walked but I would just have to manage. Standing up and straightening my jacket, I looked at Raven.

"How do I look?" I asked.

"A bit frumpy, but it just looks like a dress under a jacket, I don't think anyone will take too much notice of those clothes," she said. "You need to try and clean your legs though, there's dried blood all down them."

"And you need to pull your hair round over your shoulders to cover that up," Jude said, leaning into me. "It looks like a love bite gone horribly wrong."

I pulled my hair round, running my fingers through the knotted strands, trying to smooth it out.

"Is that better?" I asked, trying to cover Carly's bite mark the best I could.

"That's fine, just make sure you keep your hair covered over it," said Max, looking more like a biker now he had on jeans, a leather jacket, and black boots. He flicked his blond hair from out of his eyes. "I'm gonna check the rest of these lockers and see if I can find us some I.D. cards."

"I just need a shirt or jacket," said Jude, "and then we can go." He stood in ripped jeans that were slightly too long for him.

"Try this," I said, handing him a dark blue shirt that had been screwed up at the bottom of a locker.

He put it on. It was a little too tight but made his body look good, his muscles clearly defined through the fabric.

"Hey, Kassidy," he whispered. "Just so you know, I don't bite like Carly." He grinned at me. His blue eyes sparkled a mischievous glint.

"That's not even funny, Jude," I glared. "She nearly killed me."

"I'm just teasing." He looked at me with sorry eyes. "I'm trying to lighten up the moment after all the shit we've gone through."

"Nothing's gonna lighten up the moment. Even if we get out of here, what are we gonna do about the crap travelling through our veins?" I asked.

"Let's worry about that later," said Max. "I can't find any I.D. cards so I guess we'll have to escape without them."

"I found one in this locker," smiled Jude, waving it around.

"Let's have a look..." started Raven, but she stopped abruptly. "I can hear footsteps".

The room fell into silence as we listened to the *tap, tap, tap* of shoes walking on the tiled floor of the corridor outside. My heart started to pick up pace again. When was this nightmare gonna be over?

Jude crept over to the door and peered out through the tiny gap.

"Who is it?" whispered Raven, fear clouding her eyes. "Please don't let it be the Cleaners, please." She closed her eyes and grabbed hold of my hand.

"Shhh," glared Jude. "It looks like a hospital porter."

"Is it a normal porter or a *dead* porter?" whispered Raven, her eyes still screwed shut.

"What the fuck…" Jude turned and scowled at Raven. "He looks very much alive to me."

Raven opened one eye and looked at us. "You never know in this place."

"Has he gone?" whispered Max, trying to see over Jude's shoulder.

"No, he's heading this way," said Jude. "Hide behind the lockers, quick."

Raven hesitated. I pulled on her hand, dragging her behind a row of lockers. We stood in silence. The door swung open and in walked the porter.

CHAPTER NINETEEN

I peeked around the edge of the locker. The porter had stopped in the middle of the room, fumbling through his pocket. Taking out a bunch of keys, he walked over to a large cupboard and unlocked the door. He turned suddenly and caught sight of me peering at him.

"I know your there, come out," he ordered, walking toward my hiding place.

I looked at Raven. She stood cowering behind me. Her eyes wide with fear.

I stepped out from behind the locker so as not to give away Raven hiding there.

"You're one of those volunteers who's escaped, aren't you?" he said. He pulled out a knife from his pocket and waved it in front of me.

I recognised the porter. It was Fred Butler who had given me the soup on Ward 2.

"They say you're infected, dangerous." He waved the knife again, stepping a little nearer.

"I'm not dangerous. All I want to do is get out of here and never come back." I held up my hands as if to show I meant him no harm. "Look at me, I'm just a nineteen-year-old girl – do I really look dangerous?"

He scoffed. "Not dangerous, huh? I've heard what you and your group of mates did to poor Nurse Jones – look at the state of you – her blood is still on you." His eyes wandered down my legs and he took another step toward me.

"That's not her blood. I didn't do anything to Nurse Jones. It was those freaky things you've got here that killed her – those Cleaners."

"*Cleaners*," Fred chuckled. "Cleaners clean – they don't kill the staff or patients – you think I'm daft or something? I guess now you're gonna tell me it wasn't you and your mates that butchered the other volunteers up on Ward 2. I've seen what you did to one of them – what you *left* of one of them."

"That *wasn't* us!" I snapped. "They turned on each other, they tried to kill me – this is their blood on my legs. Whatever Doctor Middleton injected into us – it turned half the group into monsters."

"Well I guess you can tell the police that when they lock you away into the loony–bin – where killers like you are kept," he spat. Waving the knife, he motioned for me to head toward the door. "Move."

"I'm *not* going anywhere with you." I stood firm. "We haven't killed anyone and if it's the loony-bin you think I should be in then you may as well leave me here – 'cos that's exactly what this place is."

Fred slashed the knife through the air – inches from my face. I backed away, hitting the row of lockers that Raven hid behind, knocking the chair leg over that Max had placed there. Snatching it up I waved it through the air.

"Keep back," I snapped. I grabbed a small metal pole from off the floor and placed it over the wooden chair leg so it resembled a cross. Maybe Fred would shrink away like the Cleaners had back in the kitchen? Shoving it in front of Fred's face, I waited for him to shrivel back – fade away, but he didn't. The cross had no effect on him whatsoever. From the corner of my eye, I saw Jude and Max. They raced at Fred from behind – Max clinging hold of Fred's neck – Jude punching him in the side of his face. I rushed forward – smacking the knife from Fred's hand with the metal pole – sending it spiralling across the room.

"Get him to the floor!" Jude shouted, aiming his fist toward Fred's stomach. He punched him. Max lost his grip and toppled back.

"You're gonna have to do better than that, lads," growled Fred, smacking his fist into Jude's face – launching him into the wall. Fred turned and kicked out – his boot thudded into Max's cheek. Spinning around, Fred ran for the knife. I had to stop him – I had to get to the knife before he did. I threw myself across the room. I landed on the floor and slid across the cold tiles. Fred clattered into me – our hands snatching for the knife. I felt the back of his hand strike my face and I fell back.

"You want the knife, girly?" he spat. "I'll give you the knife."

The blade glinted as it was thrust toward me but stopped just before it reached my throat. I looked up, surprised to see Raven standing over Fred – her black-claw-like nails dug into his neck. She lifted him off the floor with ease. He hung in the air, legs flopping about like they were on elastic. Surprised at Raven's strength, I stood up – mouth hung open.

"Raven, how can you do…?" I stopped mid-sentence. Raven's eyes had turned black, her face full of anger. Jude and Max now stood – eyes wide.

"What the hell…?" Max whispered, walking around slowly, staring up into Raven's face.

"Hey, Raven. Can you hear me?" Jude asked, clicking his fingers in front of her face.

She seemed to snap out of her trance-like state, and realising what she was doing, she gasped and dropped Fred to the floor. Throwing her hands up to her face, Raven backed away.

Fred lay unconscious, his body sprawled across the floor.

"Help me tie him up. We need to secure him with something," Max said, rolling Fred onto his front and pulling his arms round to his back.

I looked around the floor. There was so much rubbish but nothing to use to tie Fred up with.

"Check the cupboard that Fred opened, there might be something in there," Jude said, frantically searching the lockers but finding nothing.

I searched the top shelf. It was full of candles and bars of soap. The second shelf had boxes of tools, and it was in one of them I found two rolls of thick duct tape. Taking them out, I handed them to Jude. Turning back to the cupboard, I continued to search the last two shelves. There was nothing worth taking, and as I went to walk away, I noticed four photographs stuck to the inside of the cupboard door. They were photos of staff members. Porters and domestic workers from past years. The first two had 1980 written on the back. The third was from 1984 and the last one I snatched from off the cupboard door. Stunned, I checked the date on the back – 1996. Shaking my head, I took another look at the faces in the photo. Standing amongst the staff was my dad.

CHAPTER TWENTY

I stared at the photo. Had I made a mistake? No – it was definitely my dad. A feeling of dread filled the pit of my stomach at the realisation that he had worked here – at Cruor Pharma. I flipped the photo over and checked the date again. 1996. I would have been only one year old – too young to remember. Thoughts of my childhood swam around in my mind as I tried to think back – search my memories, but no matter how hard I tried, the earliest memories were of play school and my dad forgetting to pick me up after downing his usual bottle of whiskey. I couldn't remember ever seeing him go to work.

I was stirred from my thoughts by a low moaning noise. Fred was rousing – his mouth had been stuffed with a screwed up piece of dirty material. Jude and Max had secured his arms tight behind him and had taped his ankles together with the duct tape. Raven sat on a wooden bench staring at her hands, turning them over as if in search of some explanation as to how she had got the strength to lift a man up with one hand. I folded the photograph in half and placed it in my pocket. I didn't want the others to see it. How would they react if they found out that my dad had worked here? Would they treat me differently – not trust me? It wasn't just those thoughts that plagued my mind. I felt a kind of shame knowing that my dad had worked for such a place. Had he known the horrors that went on here? If he had then I couldn't even bear the thought of it, it was too horrific to comprehend.

"It's time we left," said Max, hoisting Fred up against the wall. "Who knows when someone will come looking for Fred. He'll be missed by someone soon, and I don't want to be here when they come looking."

"Is everyone ready?" asked Jude, looking at each of us in turn. "We don't want any fuck-ups. Do you know where to go when we get out of here, Kassidy?"

I thought back to Ben, his directions to the chapel played through my mind. "I think so." I nodded my head.

"I hope so," said Max, looking at me with a worried expression over his face. "When we get outside we don't want to hang around."

Not wanting Fred to hear where we were heading, I whispered the way to the chapel to the others.

"Let's go then," said Max, walking toward the door.

Raven stood up. "Here, take these," she hissed at me, shoving the iPod and passport that

I had taken from Ward 1 into my hands. "I'm not carrying dead people's belongings so they can follow me about and haunt me." She turned away and followed Max to the door.

"Better not argue with her," winked Jude, "You don't want to end up like Fred over there."

I looked at Fred. His eyes were open and he stared back. He mumbled something at Jude but it sounded like a load of nonsense to me. Probably pissed off that Max and Jude had tied him up.

I crouched down in front of Fred, and checking over my shoulder to make sure the others couldn't hear me, I whispered, "Did you know Robert Bell? He's my dad." Fred nodded his head slowly. "Did you work with him?" Another nod from Fred. "Did he know about the drug trials?"

Before Fred could nod or shake his head, Jude tapped me on the shoulder.

"Come on, Kassidy, we have to go," he said, glaring at Fred. "There's no point talking to him. He's one of them, he tried to stab you with that knife, remember?"

I stood up – down-hearted. I wanted to know more. I wanted to ask Fred if my dad was a part of these awful drug trials. Fred mumbled again. His eyes angry. I bent down and went to pull out the dirty material from Fred's mouth but Jude grabbed my arm and pulled it away.

"We don't have time, Kassidy," he said. "If you take that material out from his mouth, he'll start screaming and shouting and letting everyone in this building know where we are. Leave him."

Reluctantly, I walked away.

Pushing open the door and checking to see if the corridor was clear, Max stepped out followed by Raven. I shoved the iPod and passport into my jacket pocket.

"You go in front," said Max, looking at me. "You know the way."

Turning left down the corridor, I followed it round to the old fire exit. Taking the rusty key from my pocket, I slipped it into the lock.

"Shit," whispered Jude from behind me. "I've left that I.D. card back in the locker room. Wait here while I go get it."

"Hurry up", said Max. "I just want to get out of here."

Jude turned back and disappeared round the corridor. We waited nervously. Butterflies churned away inside my stomach. I was scared that something other than Jude might come back round the corridor and catch us, and then there was the fear of what we might find outside. Raven suddenly slumped down against the wall.

Her eyes had rolled back in their sockets and her mouth hung open.

"Raven, what's wrong?" I asked, crouching down beside her. She didn't answer. I took hold of her shoulders and gently shook her. She flopped over to the right like an unconscious drunk.

"Max, help me," I said. "I don't know what's wrong with her."

He knelt down beside me and held Raven's chin, tilting her head up.

"Can you hear me, Raven?" he asked. "It's Max."

Jude suddenly appeared from around the corner waving the I.D. badge about. "Got it", he smiled. His eyes darkened when he saw Raven. "What's wrong with her now?"

"She just collapsed," I said.

"Let me take a look," said Jude, pushing me aside. He took hold of her shoulders and shook her roughly. "Raven, wake up."

"Careful, Jude," whispered Max. "You don't want to make her worse."

Raven suddenly let out a sigh. "You took your time," she hissed, glaring at Jude, her eyes now staring angrily at him.

"What the hell...?" whispered Max, "Raven, you just collapsed and now you're acting like nothing happened."

She looked at Max confused. "What? I don't remember."

"Do you feel okay now?" I asked, helping her back up onto her feet.

Raven stood and shrugged her shoulders. "I feel fine. Just fed up with having to wait for him to come back. We could have been outside by now." She glared at Jude.

"I couldn't find the I.D. at first," said Jude, frowning at Raven. "It had fallen on the floor. I must have dropped it when we were fighting with Fred. Look what else I have though." He waved another I.D. badge about, a big grin on his face.

"Where did you find that?" I asked, knowing that Max had searched the locker room earlier for I.D. badges.

"It's Fred's," Jude smiled. "I'm sure he won't mind us borrowing it. I took it from his pocket. You can use it, Max. There's no point in Raven or Kassidy having it with a man's name written across the front."

"Thanks," said Max, taking it from Jude. "Now let's get out of here."

I turned back to the fire exit. Gripping hold of the key, I turned it slowly. The lock was stiff and it creaked as the key went round. A sharp click and the lock opened. Taking hold of the handle, I pulled down. The door groaned on its hinges. I held my breath as I felt the cold morning air against my skin.

CHAPTER TWENTY ONE

Hidden from view under the large oak tree, we stood in silence. The dark, menacing atmosphere of the hospital that had haunted my steps had lifted a little. And although the relief of escaping to the outside felt like a victory, I knew that there was still trouble to come. A dense fog hung lifelessly over Strangers Hill and the grounds of Cruor Pharma, like smoke trapped under a glass dome. Apart from the odd crow screeching overhead, there was nothing but a deathly silence.

I peered through the drooping branches. Another week or two and the trees would be bare, with autumn approaching. The ground was a soggy mess of fallen leaves and mud from the storm last night. The leaves stuck to my shoes like wet sheets of paper.

"I can't see a thing," I whispered. "The fog is too thick." I turned round and looked at the others.

"You said we had to follow the path to the left," whispered Max. "We can see the ground so the path should be easy enough to follow."

"What if someone comes?" hissed Raven. "We won't be able to see them until it's too late."

She hugged her arms tight across her chest, shivering.

"It works both ways," said Jude. "They won't spot *us* until it's too late."

"Let's go then," whispered Max, thrusting his hands into the leather jacket he had found, trying to keep them warm.

"Shhh," I hushed. "Can you hear something?"

We stood still. Max shook his head as if to say he'd heard nothing. Raven had frozen – eyes wide. Jude suddenly pointed to our right. Heavy footsteps were squelching toward the oak tree. There was nowhere to hide other than under the tree so we waited – hoping that whoever it was would pass by. Crouching down, I held my breath as a pair of booted feet stopped just on the other side of the branches. A waft of cigarette smoke filtered through.

Someone spoke. A male. "Can't see any sign of them, boss. They must still be inside the hospital. Me and Charlie have walked around the perimeter several times over the last few hours and not caught sight of one of them."

Another voice. This one crackling as if coming via a radio. *"Keep walking, Steve. You don't stop until someone has found them."*

"I don't know why the police don't get called in to deal with them?" asked Steve.

"Doctor Middleton wants this kept quiet, the police still haven't forgotten the last time some of the volunteers escaped. No one wants this getting messy," the second voice hissed and crackled again.

"I didn't work here when that happened, but I've heard the stories. Doctor Middleton had to pay out a bit to the local police in Holly Tree, didn't he?" asked Steve.

"He paid out big. Inspector Cropper wasn't gonna stay quiet without a bribe," the voice hissed.

"Did they ever catch the three volunteers who escaped?"

"Only one... Sylvia Green. It was too late for Middleton to get his hands on her though. Derbyshire police caught her when she tried to kill herself jumping off Millers Dale Bridge. She got sectioned under the mental health act and sent to Curden Mental Institute."

"I bet Middleton shit himself," sniggered Steve.

"Not really. The girl was written off as insane. Whatever she said about this place, no one believed her."

"I guess I'd better keep looking then," said Steve. His cigarette dropped to the ground by his boots and he crushed it into the wet, muddy leaves.

"Keep me up to date, Steve, if you see any of them. Make sure you keep your radio on, just in case I need to get hold of you."

"Will do, boss," answered Steve, the sound of static filling the quiet morning.

We watched from under the tree as Steve strolled away, following the path to the left – the way we needed to go. When he had disappeared into the fog, I turned to face the others.

"Let's give him five minutes to get well ahead of us. I don't fancy bumping into him or his mate Charlie," I whispered.

"At least they still think we're inside the hospital," Max said. "Did you hear what they said about the other volunteers? My brother might be one of those who escaped."

"Let's hope so," I smiled. I pulled out the passport in my pocket and opened it up onto the page with Sylvia Green's photo on. "Look, this is Sylvia's passport. I have her consent form from Cruor Pharma in the back. Do you think if we escape we could help her? Get her out of that mental hospital?"

"No chance," said Jude, looking over my shoulder at the passport. "You heard what they said, she's gone mad. There's nothing we can do to change that. And anyway, they'd never let us in to see her."

"She shouldn't be locked up in there. It's not her fault. Whatever happened to Sylvia here is the reason she tried to take her own life. I bet she isn't even mad. No one believes her because what happens in this place is just too far-fetched – unbelievable. But it's all true," I snapped. "What she says *sounds* crazy to the outside world but to us and the other volunteers, it's real."

"Calm down, Kassidy," Jude smiled, taking my hand. "What's the point in even talking about this now, we haven't even escaped out of the grounds yet."

I pulled my hand away – anger flared up inside of me. This whole situation was wrong. This place was fucked up and the local police didn't care as long as they were getting a payoff. I was about to tell Jude to shut the hell up when I noticed the grey nails on my right hand. They looked more like claws – like Raven's did. Yanking up the sleeve of my jacket, the black veins had spread down to my wrist and twisted round the top of my hand, like a coiled, venomous snake. The sight of it brought me back down to earth and I felt my anger fade. Jude was right. What was the point of planning to free Sylvia when we weren't even free ourselves?

I took another look at my hand. What could I do apart from let it take its course? I couldn't stop this drug from travelling through my body. I was helpless. But I could still get out of here – escape. I wasn't going to let Middleton have me. I would do whatever it took to get away from him, the Cleaners, and the police.

Pulling the branches aside, I peered through the fog. There was no sign of Steve. I looked at the others. "Let's go".

Stepping out into the open, I felt uncovered – exposed, but at least with the fog it gave us some shelter from anyone or anything watching from the hospital windows. I looked up at the building with its crumbly, vine-covered walls, broken windows, and missing roof tiles. It towered over us. Through the fog it almost seemed to be waiting to pounce –capturing us forever amongst its vile grip. Its evil history kept well hidden from the main entrance where I had waited in line yesterday. I remembered how nervous I had felt when faced with the building of Cruor Pharma with its barred windows and overbearing structure – its unfriendly – clinical appearance. But I'd take that half of Cruor Pharma any day, than have to endure this part of the building ever again.

Keeping close together, we followed the path to the left. I recalled Ben telling me to look out for some steps that led down a slope. After five minutes of walking I was beginning to think we had missed them when I suddenly spotted a break in the path.

"There's the steps," I hushed, not wanting to make too much noise. We huddled at the top. The first two steps were all I could see. They were worn and broken and looked slippery from the damp air.

"I don't like this," hissed Raven. "It looks like we're stepping into something unnatural. Who knows what's at the bottom of these steps."

"It can't be any worse than what we've already seen," I whispered, although I had to admit, it did look like we were walking into the unknown.

"Let's not hang around. Keep going and watch yourself on these steps," said Max, walking in front and leading the way. "At least we're that bit further away from the hospital. The greater distance we put between us and that place, the better."

I turned around and looked back at the hospital. All I could see was a dark blotch through the fog where the hospital stood. Turning to face the steps, I saw Jude disappear into the murky haze. Max and Raven had already vanished – swallowed up in the fog. Taking my time – careful not to slip on the stone steps, I reached the bottom.

"Which way is it?" asked Max, pushing his damp, blonde hair from out of his eyes.

"We go right and follow the path until we come to the chapel," I whispered. "I don't think it's too much further."

"Look, there's someone at the top of the steps," pointed Jude, head tilted up.

A cone of light swooped about – the beam not strong enough to reach the bottom of the steps where we stood. Whoever was holding the torch couldn't be seen through the fog. Muffled voices filtered through the haze – it was Steve and someone else – probably his security guard mate, Charlie. They were still searching for us.

We kept still, afraid that if we continued down the path they would hear our footsteps on the gravel track.

"I've been down these steps five times already through the night," moaned Steve, "I'm bloody cold and damp. I just want to get back indoors, warm up, and eat my pastry – I'm starving."

"Me too, mate," said Charlie. "I've got a nice pork pie waiting for me and a Pot Noodle to warm me up, but the boss ain't gonna let us in until those volunteers are found. This night shift has been nothing but a fucking headache, and I bet they won't let us go home at the end of the shift either. The police will have to be called in sooner or later."

"What do you think they'll do with the volunteers when they catch them?" asked Steve.

"Who gives a shit? I don't. Serves them right for being greedy little fuckers. Why don't they get a job like the rest of us? These kids want everything for doing nothing. They make me sick," spat Charlie.

"Yeah, but, come on – you wouldn't want your daughter coming in here and getting messed up – no one deserves that," said Steve. "If my daughter signed up for some drug test I wouldn't expect her to come out all messed up, or the police trying to cover it up – that ain't right."

"Nothing's right about this place, but I wanna keep my job. There's no other work in Holly Tree. This is as good as it gets. I keep my head down and my mouth shut – you can't go wrong. What goes on behind these walls stays behind these walls," said Charlie. "I've heard some of the other staff gossip about this place – sends shivers right through me."

"What gossip?" asked Steve.

"Shit you wouldn't believe. Some say it's haunted. Some say it's got deranged patients wandering the old corridors, others say the doctors aren't like us," whispered Charlie.

"What do you mean – not like us?" said Steve.

"Middleton, Wright, Fletcher, and Middleton's son. I dunno, there's something weird about them," hushed Charlie.

I wanted to give them a round of applause. I had only spent a night here and it hadn't taken me long to figure out that Middleton and the others weren't right, yet these two security guards who had probably worked here for a while were only just getting it. And who was Middleton's son? That was twice now I had heard him be mentioned but still had no idea who he was.

"You mean like aliens?" asked Steve.

"Not fucking aliens, you dick," said Charlie. "I mean…"

The sound of static cut through the fog as a voice came over Steve's radio. It made me jump.

"Steve, get Charlie and make your way to the locker room."

"The locker room?" asked Steve. "That's in the old part of the hospital, isn't it, boss?"

"Yeah, meet me at the front entrance and I'll show you the way. Fred Butler's been murdered."

"What… how… by who?" asked Steve, his voice shaky.

I looked at Max, then Jude and Raven. I couldn't believe what I was hearing. Fred was very much alive when we had left him.

"Those volunteers, that's who. Fred was found all taped up – his throat has been slit. Middleton's going mad. If we don't find those volunteers soon, Middleton will be after our blood I reckon. Hurry up and get round here – we'll need to stick together if we're going into the old hospital."

"Shit," I heard Charlie say. "What the fuck are they injecting these volunteers with?"

I looked down at the black, lumpy veins covering the back of my hand and thought the same thing.

"That's not for us to know, Charlie. We just keep the outside secure."

"Then why are we being sent inside? We don't patrol in there," huffed Charlie.

"We're not patrolling... we're moving the body. Middleton wants us to tidy Fred up – make him look like he had some kind of accident."

"A cover-up you mean, boss?" asked Steve, the sound of static cutting through the fog.

"Looks like it. Just get your arses over here now."

The hissing of the radio cut out. The torchlight moved away from the steps. Steve's and Charlie's voices disappeared into the thick, stagnant fog.

"So now we're getting blamed for someone else's murder," said Max, blowing warm air over his cold hands. "Fred already accused us of killing Nurse Jones and the other volunteers – now he's part of the body count."

"Who do you think killed him?" whispered Raven. "Do you think we're next?"

"I don't think they want us dead. Doctor Fletcher said something about us being a miracle breakthrough. But if Middleton got his hands on us, then he would ruin us," I whispered.

"Why set us up for murder then?" said Jude. "If we get locked away for all these deaths then Middleton won't be able to have us. It doesn't make sense."

"Nothing makes sense in this *hell*," hissed Raven. "We're all doomed, we're gonna spend the rest of eternity wandering the corridors of death."

"Ever heard of the word *hope*, Raven?" snapped Jude. "We might as well go and hand ourselves in if we are to believe you."

"You were the last one to see Fred Butler – did you kill him?" hissed Raven, backing away from Jude.

"Why would I kill him?" Jude spat. "If I wanted him dead I could've killed Fred when we were wrapping duct tape around him. Don't you think there's more fucked-up things wandering around that hospital than me?"

"Let's not start turning on each other," I said. "There's no reason for Jude to have killed him, Raven. We aren't killers – we're victims."

Raven stood still, a look of distrust across her face. "I don't trust any of you." She pointed her finger at us. "You all told me on Ward 2 that everything was okay – but look at us now – ruined – fated."

"We will be fated if we don't get moving," whispered Max.

"I'm not waiting around here anymore, I'm going to the chapel," I sighed, fed up with Raven's outbursts and feeling a little pissed off at being told I wasn't trusted. I felt like pointing out to her that she was more like those freaks inside the hospital than any of us. So should we trust her? I looked at Jude. He stood shaking his head, his blue eyes troubled. I couldn't imagine him slitting anyone's throat. No, we were all victims – Middleton's prey – all four of us.

As I turned to follow the path toward the chapel, Jude spoke up.

"Let's just make a run for it, fuck the chapel," he said. "It sounds like the security guards will have their hands full inside with old Fred. The gate might be unmanned."

"I don't think so," said Max. "A place like this would never leave the gates unattended – it's too risky."

"I think we should just stick to the plan," I said. "Let's wait in the chapel, sort out how we're going to walk through those gates, and what direction we're going head in when we get out."

"*If* we get out," hissed Raven, pushing past me. "I'm going to the chapel – it's a place of peace. Maybe our souls will be saved from all these *dead things*. Maybe there's some holy water and crucifixes in there."

"You think that shit is gonna get you out of here?" scoffed Jude.

"Well the police sure ain't gonna help us," hissed Raven. "You heard what those two security guards said – the police are freaking bent as hell."

I'd heard enough. I didn't want to stand out here in the fog any longer, listening to Jude and Raven bitch at each other, so I continued to follow the path toward the chapel. My head was close to bursting. I didn't know if going to the chapel was the right thing to do, but so far, everything Ben had told me to do had worked out okay, and even though Raven seemed crazy with her strange thoughts and ideas about the dead – one thing she had said, did seem plausible. The accidental cross I had made back in the kitchen with the knife and ladle had had some kind of effect against the Cleaners. It hadn't worked on Fred Butler, but maybe that was because he was just like us – alive – or at least, he was when we'd left him in the locker room. A chapel must have crosses and crucifixes, I thought. If I found any, I would definitely be stuffing the pockets of my jacket with as many as I could.

The black-shadowy mass of the hospital had disappeared. A steep embankment rose over the path to my right, blocking any view of Cruor Pharma. I knew we hadn't travelled too far down Strangers Hill, probably not even a quarter of it. If we made it through the gates we would have some trek before we reached the bottom, and probably a further ten minutes' walk to Holly Tree. I scoffed at my thoughts. Walk – I wasn't gonna walk – I'm gonna *freaking run*. Run for my life.

"Hey, Kass," Max whispered, catching me up. "Don't let Raven get to you with all her talk about death and hell and us not making it out of here. She's just strange and believes in all that weird stuff."

"She is strange," I said, nodding my head. "But maybe we're getting pissed off with her because we don't want to admit that perhaps she's right. Maybe we can't face the truth. Maybe we're all just hoping that we'll wake up and this has been a horrible nightmare. The fact is, we've seen things that we never believed in – things we can't explain – and it's easier to pretend aren't real. But no matter how many times I look at my veins – the truth is still there."

I looked at Max. He walked beside me, his head hung low.

"I guess you're right," he mumbled. "I don't even know where to begin. What have we seen? Zombies? Ghosts? Vampires?" He took a deep breath. "Where do we go when we get out of here? Can we go back to our normal lives? Probably not. Who do we trust?"

I placed my hand on his arm and gently squeezed. "I don't know any more than you do. All I've got is questions and no answers and a head full of hideous images. Oh, and let's not forget, things that can go through doors and doctors with multiple personalities."

"Things really do go bump in the night at this place." Max forced a smile. "Whatever happens, I'm glad you're with me. If I was left with just Raven and Jude, I think I would have lost all hope and my sanity."

I smiled. "Thanks, Max, I'm glad you're with me too."

We carried on walking until the path split into two directions. An old broken sign hung lifelessly from a wooden stake pushed into the mud. It read *To the Chapel*. We waited for Jude and Raven to catch up. Their gravelly footsteps could be heard before we saw them appear through the fog.

"This way," I whispered.

"Good," huffed Raven. "Maybe we'll be safe in there?"

Jude hung back. He hesitated – still reluctant with the plan of hiding out in the chapel.

"Who says that the chapel is going to be any safer than being out here?" he said. "We've only got Fletcher's word on it and I don't trust him. He stuck that fucking needle in you and pumped your body with a drug that's turned half the volunteers into crazed zombie-things." He pointed his finger at me. "I don't get it. Why are you trusting him?"

I shrugged my shoulders. "Because he's been the only one to help and so far it's got us here – to the chapel. If he hadn't have given me that key, then we'd still be stuck inside the hospital."

"Listen, Jude, if you really don't want to wait in the chapel you could always try and get through the gate by yourself. You don't have to wait for us," said Max, plumes of cold breath floating from his lips.

"I don't want us to split up," said Jude. "We're stronger together."

"Fine, then let's keep going," I said, walking away down the path. I just wanted to get inside – out of the freezing fog. My legs looked blue with the cold.

We continued a short way until a dark shape emerged through the fog. The path came to a sudden end. Tucked in the side of Strangers Hill and hidden amongst a crop of tall fir trees was the chapel.

CHAPTER TWENTY TWO

The chapel, shrouded in fir trees and fog, looked forgotten and neglected. Its grey stones, which were crumbling with moss and ivy, had seen better days. Stinging nettles and weeds grew in thick clumps around its foundations like they were a part of the chapel. It made me feel sad somehow. Lonely. The two arched windows on either side of the front door were covered in grime – its stained-glass pictures unrecognisable.

"Wow, this place couldn't have been used for years," whispered Max, his eyes wandering over the deserted building. "I wonder when the last time that bell got rung?"

I followed his gaze up to a small tower. The rusty bell hung lifelessly.

"Not for a very long time, judging by the state of this place," I sighed, that feeling of sadness creeping through me.

"What do you expect in an evil place like this? The dead have no need for such a building. It's probably been turned into the *devil's lair*," hissed Raven.

Max looked at me. He rolled his eyes in response to Raven's comments.

"Are you sure you want to go in?" asked Jude. "It looks unfriendly – like it doesn't want us here."

Max sniggered. "Jude, you sound like Raven."

"What I mean is... oh, just forget it." He turned away, embarrassed to be classed like Raven.

"Let's go in," I said, stepping carefully through the stinging nettles toward the wooden door. As I approached the arched entrance, I felt suddenly anxious. I brushed the feeling away. Raven's and Jude's comments were playing on my mind. This was a chapel for goodness sake – a place of safety, I told myself. I reached out and took hold of the iron handle. It creaked and groaned as I twisted it round. The iron latch clunked as it freed itself from years of neglect and the wooden door – reluctant to move – slowly grumbled open. A cold, icy blast hit me – knocking me back into Max. He caught me before I fell to the floor. The sound of rasping whispers flew past me, caught up in the icy blast.

"Get out... you are not welcome... be gone..." the whispers hissed.

"Did you hear that?" I asked, turning to the others.

"What?" whispered Max, his arms still holding me up.

"Something said we aren't welcome. It told us to go." I shivered in his arms.

"It was just the wind whistling through the chapel as you opened up the door," said Max. "That's all I heard."

"Did you hear it?" I looked over Max's shoulder at Raven and Jude.

They both shook their heads.

Slipping from Max's hold, I cautiously stepped inside. There was nothing but silence. Whatever I'd heard was now gone. It couldn't have been the wind – there was no wind. The air outside was filled with a stagnant fog – nothing stirred in the stillness. Something had hit me but now the atmosphere seemed calm – the mood suddenly peaceful.

It was semi-dark inside the chapel. The approaching morning light didn't do much to brighten the space. There were two stained-glass windows on each side of the chapel. The centre aisle led up to a wooden lectern and three rows of pews were lined on either side. Large, thick cobwebs hung from the ceiling like threadbare material, which clung to my arms as I pushed them aside like I was opening curtains. The air was filled with dust and the smell of decay was strong.

"I feel sick," Jude mumbled. "The smell in here is rotten. I'm gonna sit by the door and get some fresh air." He slumped down on the floor, holding his head in his hands.

I bent down next to him, squeezing his shoulder with my hand. He looked up at me. His eyes looked dark and cloudy and his face had broken out into a sweat.

"Show me your arm," I said, fearing that maybe Jude had been given VA20 like the rest of us after all and it was only now taking effect.

He pushed his shirt sleeve up to the elbow but there were no signs of black, lumpy veins.

"Shall I see if I can find you something to lay your head on?" I asked, feeling his forehead. He was burning a fever. His head felt like a hot water bottle.

"Yes," he sighed, leaning against the wall.

I stood up. Raven and Max looked worried. They both had their hands covering their noses, blocking the rancid stench that filled the air.

"Is he gonna turn into one of those zombie-things?" Raven asked, twisting a strand of her black greasy hair around her finger.

"I've checked his arm. There are no black veins like ours," I said. "But he looks really ill. We should keep an eye on him. That's all we can do for now."

Walking down the aisle, I stopped at the first row of pews. They were lined with prayer cushions. Taking one, I dusted it off and handed it to Max.

"Give this to Jude to lie on," I said. "It might make him feel more comfortable."

"I think I'm gonna sit down for a bit," said Raven, knocking the dust from some of the prayer cushions. She plonked herself down. "I'm so tired. I think I could sleep for a year."

"Me too," said Max. "We've been up all night. No wonder Jude's feeling ill, he's probably knackered. I know I could do with a good sleep, something to eat, and I've got a raging thirst."

"I'm thirsty, too," murmured Raven, her eyes shut. She'd put her legs up onto a pew and her head rested against a pile of cushions.

"How long do you think we have before the night shift changes over?" I asked, looking at Max.

"Probably another hour," he shrugged. "We need to decide how we're going to walk through those gates with the rest of the staff unnoticed."

"Well, you and Jude have an I.D. badge each," I said, "So maybe Raven should walk out with Jude and I'll go out with you. If you hold up the I.D. badge for the security guards to see then I might be able to just slip through."

"Go out in pairs you mean?" he said. "Yeah, it's probably best not to go in a group, we'd stand out too much – we know their looking for three of us at least."

"I just hope that Jude is well enough to walk," I said, looking over at the door where he lay.

"And run," Max whispered. "We might have to run."

I nodded my head. The thought of having to walk past the security guards pretending to be a member of staff filled me with dread. Would we pull it off?

"Hey, we'll do it," said Max, as if able to read my mind. "We have to."

"If we make it past the gates, where should we head?" I asked. "We need a direction. We don't want to look suspicious – we've got to act like all those other workers leaving work. We can't catch the bus – we've no money."

Max sat down on a pew, picked up an ancient-looking bible that lay on the floor and waved it in front of his face, trying to rid the smell that hung in the chapel. "Holly Tree is the nearest town and most of the staff come from there. So, we take the path along the road that leads down to the bottom of Strangers Hill but we don't follow it all the way. As soon as we're out of sight of Cruor Pharma and out of sight from the staff leaving, we get off that path and cut down the hill under the cover of the trees."

"Then what?" I asked. "Do we go into Holly Tree, and if so, where do we go when we get into town? Will we be safe there?"

"The only people looking for us at the moment are staff members from Cruor Pharma, and they still think we're inside the hospital," said Max. "The police don't know about us yet which gives us a bit of a head start, but when Middleton realises we're out, that's when he'll go to the police – to Inspector Cropper – that's when we'll need to be out of Holly Tree."

"Was it Inspector Cropper who dealt with you when you went to the police about your brother?" I asked.

Max nodded his head. "Yeah. No wonder he wasn't interested. He's probably on Middleton's payroll. I bet he was pleased when he thought he'd pulled the wool over my eyes and got rid of me."

"I wonder what he would've done if you'd been persistent?" I whispered.

We both looked at each other as if thinking the same thought.

"Guess I wouldn't be here now talking to you," sighed Max, running his fingers through his hair. He leant back against the pew slowly shaking his head. "Shit, I'd probably be dead or locked up somewhere."

"Do you really think the police would do that – kill anyone who might give up their secret with Cruor Pharma and Middleton?" I whispered, a bad feeling churning away inside of me.

"You'd like to think that they wouldn't," he shrugged. "But who knows how deep the police are involved in all this. Inspector Cropper certainly seems to have his hands dirty. I'm sure he wouldn't want this getting out – not if he's been taking money from Middleton."

"Well at least we know not to go strolling into the Holly Tree police Station," I said. "But where do we go?"

"Jude said he has a car parked outside that bar – The Fallen Star. I think we should get the car and get the hell out of Holly Tree," said Max.

"My friend Hannah lives close by – in the next town. We could go there after we get the car. She'd help us. We could clean up and I know she'd lend me some money," I said.

"I don't know. Can you trust her?" asked Max. "Does she have anything to do with Cruor Pharma or any family that works here?"

"I trust her with my life. We've been friends since I was little," I said. "She works at the bank in The Mumbles. Her parents moved away a year ago, I've never known them to work for Cruor Pharma – ever."

A sudden doubt flashed up in my mind – my dad. I had never known my dad to work, let alone work for Cruor Pharma. Could Hannah's parents have ever worked here? No, her mum had been a librarian and her dad had worked for the local newspaper.

"Okay, we'll stop at Hannah's," said Max, standing up. "But only so we can clean up and borrow some money. Then we'll go. Can you drive?"

"I don't have a driving licence, but I can drive a car," I said. "Hannah gave me some lessons a while ago."

"Good," said Max heading toward the door. "I can't drive and I'm not sure if Jude is gonna be in any fit state to either. I'm gonna go and check on him."

I looked over at Raven. She was fast asleep. Good, I thought. Thinking of Raven made me remember the crosses and crucifixes. There must be some in this chapel somewhere. I walked down the aisle, knocking the cobwebs away. I checked the pews but the only items along them were prayer cushions and some bibles. It was strange to see the chapel so tidy and neat yet covered in dust and cobwebs. It was like it was waiting for the congregation to arrive. I reached the wooden lectern. A bible had been opened and a verse had been highlighted.

Covering my nose with the sleeve of my jacket, I started to read.

Peter 5:8 – Be sober-minded, be watchful. Your adversary the devil prowls around like a roaring lion, seeking someone to devour.

I noticed several pages had been bookmarked. Prayer cards were poking out from different pages and I opened up to the next one. Again, another verse had been highlighted.

James 4:7 – Submit yourselves therefore to God. Resist the devil, and he will flee from you.

I flipped through the other pages noticing the highlighted text. They were all verses about the devil. Had the priest who served this chapel known about Cruor Pharma and what strange things roamed its corridors? Had he been reading these verses from the bible to the people who came here? Or had he been reading them to himself for comfort and guidance? My head swam with thoughts of ghosts and monsters. I had seen enough through the night to change my beliefs about the supernatural but the devil…? That just seemed too crazy. Too extreme. But was it?

I closed the bible. Something shiny caught my eye. It was poking out from beneath a large pile of what looked like dirty-white material, shoved under the front pew. I bent down and picked it up. A silver cross hung from a string of wooden beads. Rosary beads. I slipped it over my head and tucked the silver cross under the jacket I wore. This might help me. I thought of the Cleaners. The bad smell making my stomach churn seemed so much stronger here. Whatever it was, was coming from under the pew. There was something else sticking out from under the large bundle of material. A brown leather strap. My head was telling me to leave it alone, that whatever was under this large pile of material should stay there and not be disturbed. I reached out. I tried to pull on the strap but it seemed to be caught on something. Giving it a harder yank, the strap came free, revealing a brown satchel. I gasped, falling back onto the floor. Attached to the strap was a hand – its fingers curled tight about it.

"Max, come here!" I shrieked, edging away from the bundle of material.

"What's wrong?" he said, running down the aisle toward me.

"I think there's someone under there." I pointed to the material. "Look."

Max knelt down beside me, covering his nose. Pinching a lump of the material between his two fingers, he slowly lifted the cloth up.

CHAPTER TWENTY THREE

The bundle of material almost seemed to ripple – like it was bobbing along on a gentle stream as Max cautiously lifted it up. Dust motes swirled up, making me choke. I waved my hands about trying to clear the air. The waft of rotting flesh made me gag.

"I know this is gonna sound really dumb, but after everything we've seen, do you think whatever is under this material is definitely dead?" I whispered, grabbing hold of Max's hand, stopping him from pulling the material any further.

He smiled nervously. "I don't think it's dumb to think that – I was wondering the same." He took a deep breath. "Ready?"

I nodded my head. "Do it".

Max pulled the cloth away. A body of a man lay curled up on its side. Its bony, fleshy fingers grasped a wooden cross. The clothes it had on were wet through from the decaying flesh.

"It's a priest," whispered Max, giving the body a poke with his fingers, making sure it wasn't suddenly going to get up.

I leant over the priest. He was still wearing his dog collar.

"How long do you think he's been here?" I whispered. "I know he's decomposing, but there's still a lot of him left intact."

Max shrugged his shoulders. "I don't know."

"I wonder what happened," I mumbled, cautiously taking the satchel from its fleshy grasp. "He must have been hiding – why else would he be curled up under the pew?"

"Let's cover him back up," said Max, pulling what was left of the material back over the priest. "Is there anything in the satchel?"

I stood up and unfastened the buckles. Peering inside, I could see a bible, money, and some other kind of book. I pulled it out.

"A journal," I said, turning it over in my hands. I read the name on the front. "Father William."

Flicking through the yellowed pages, I could see entries had been made on different dates.

"Looks like some kind of diary," whispered Max over my shoulder. "We should check it out. It might have some clue as to what was going on in this chapel and what happened to Father William."

"Okay, but let's sit near the door. I need some fresh air," I said, walking down the aisle, the smell of Father Williams's body making me want to puke.

We sat down on a pew near to one of the stained glass windows, the light was a little better there and I could see Father Williams's handwriting more clearly.

Opening up the pages, I said, "Where shall we start?"

"Somewhere in the middle," Max whispered. He shifted up close, resting his arm behind me on the back of the pew.

Turning to the centre of the journal, I took a deep breath and started to read.

CHAPTER TWENTY FOUR

1st May 2014

I fear something odd is going on here. The chapel and Cruor Pharma are not how I remember them to be. I can't quite put my finger on it. They are no longer the happy places I can recall. The staff look troubled and very few of them come to visit the chapel. Those that do, seem frightened and withdrawn.

I know the role of Cruor Pharma has changed somewhat over the years – the old hospital stands empty and the new building works more towards scientific study and developing drugs for cures. But still, the modern progression does not explain the heavy atmosphere that seems to dwell amongst the staff and grounds of this place. It's like the air has been tainted – no – infected by something dark.

I feel silly writing this. It sounds like the rumblings of an old fool but I am shocked by Doctor Middleton. Why hasn't he aged? Why does he look no older than he did all those years ago? It makes no sense to me. It isn't possible. And what about Doctor Fletcher? He still looks as young as ever. Maybe it's a new drug they've developed? No, that's just daft. No drug could do that.

Doctor Middleton was very cold towards me today. I could almost feel the hate coming from him. I didn't feel welcome. Maybe I'll try to talk to him another day soon. Perhaps I just caught him on a bad day?

Whatever is going on here, I shall do my best to serve the staff who come and see me. I hope that given time, they will trust me and realise I am here to help.

"Well, there's not much there that we don't already know," frowned Max. "Except the bit about Middleton and Fletcher not aging."

"That is weird," I whispered. "I saw a picture of Middleton in that old newspaper I picked up back inside the hospital. It was taken in 1974, I think. The picture wasn't very clear, but now after reading what Father William wrote I think that maybe he's right. Doctor Middleton still looks the same, but that was nearly forty years ago – how can that be?"

"Let's read some more," said Max, leaning over me and turning the page of the journal.

I looked down at Father Williams's handwriting and continued to read.

20th May 2014
My visitors to the chapel are dwindling. I don't know what I'm doing wrong? Is it just that

they are not a religious bunch? Perhaps I need to try harder? It's almost like they fear the chapel – or is it me they fear? But why?

I spoke to one of the porters today – Danny. He's been to the chapel a few times now. He sits at the back near the door. Keeps himself to himself. A quiet lad. He wanted to know my thoughts on spirits. I was rather taken aback – not the kind of question I would have expected from him. He seemed agitated. He kept looking over his shoulder like he was afraid that someone was listening. I have to admit – I feel rather spooked myself after some of the things he spoke of. He thinks he's seen ghosts. Black, shadowy shapes that float through doors, wandering through the old hospital. He says he's heard staff talk about a delivery of coffins containing bodies for research that turned up years ago. Apparently the rumour is that when the coffins were opened, the hospital changed – the staff changed. I don't know what to think. Ghosts and stories about coffins seem rather far-fetched to me, but what do I know? This place is strange. Each week I turn up at the chapel and it feels more forlorn than ever. I will pray for Danny. I know God will watch over him. I hope he comes back to see me.

Tomorrow I shall be stopping by Doctor Middleton's office. Maybe he'll be more talkative this time. I'm not sure if I will be bold enough to enquire the secret of his youthful looks. It may cause me some trouble if he thinks I'm sticking my nose in. I don't want him complaining to the Bishop.

"What do you think about that?" I turned and looked at Max.

"The coffin shit seems weird. If the hospital and its staff changed when those coffins were opened, then there must have been something in them but... I don't know, Kassidy," sighed Max, "It's everything I've never believed in. But we've seen some fucked up shit since we've been here and I think we have to face the fact that ghosts exist."

"When I first saw what had happened to the others on Ward 2 – you know, Wendy and Howard, I kept telling myself it was because of the VA20, that the drug had sent them insane, but..." I trailed off, my skin covered in goose bumps. "But it doesn't explain what the Cleaners are, it doesn't explain what has happened to Carly, and it certainly doesn't explain the weird behaviour of the doctors. When I was with Doctor Fletcher, one minute he was nice and then in a split second it was like he had taken on a completely different personality – like a schizophrenic."

"Read some more, the journal might give us the next piece of the jigsaw," said Max, tapping his finger on the page.

21st May 2014

What a strange meeting. Doctor Middleton seemed vacant. It was obvious right from the start that he wasn't interested in anything I had to say. Anyone would think I had the plague the way he kept his distance from me. I think the man could be suffering from some kind of mental disease. His behaviour was bizarre. There is something strange behind those eyes of his –I don't know what it is, but I don't like it. He is not the man I remember him to be. His reaction to me when I suggested that I come into the hospital to talk with the staff was panic. Then aggression when I tried to push the idea further. He made it quite clear that I was to stay in the chapel. I tried to talk to him about the old days when I would visit the patients on the wards but he seemed to have no memory of it. How could he have forgotten?

I casually slipped in a comment about how good he looked after all these years – his response was zero. He just glared back and ushered me out of his office.

I have to admit that I feel a sense of great relief now I am back inside the chapel. This is not a nice place to work. I feel more and more unease every time I have to visit Cruor Pharma. I wish this wasn't part of my parish.

I turned the page. The next few entries were missing, ripped out from the journal. So I carried on reading from the next time that Father William had written down his thoughts.

16th June 2014.
I don't know what to do? Should I send a letter to the Bishop with my concerns? No. He will think I am mad. Am I mad? This place has me doubting my sanity. I feel something. I don't know what it is? Something is pushing me away. When I walk through the gates to Cruor Pharma, it's like a shadow falls upon me. Watches me. Follows me. Am I paranoid? Maybe.

Danny came to see me. He's leaving Cruor Pharma. He looks ruined – wretched – a troubled soul. He says he hasn't slept in weeks. He's seen things. Heard things. I feel disturbed – unsettled. He told me about a drug trial. A drug trial that hadn't been authorised. It went wrong. Danny heard the screams. Saw one of the patients. It looked like – as he describes it – a zombie. I don't want to believe him. The truth scares me – has me questioning everything I have ever believed in. I told Danny he must go to the police. He doesn't want to, he's too scared. I tried to calm him. I hope he will take my advice. I must pray. The Lord will comfort me. I must have faith.

I looked at Max. "Shall I carry on?"

He nodded his head. "There might be something about my brother's drug trial. He came here three months ago, in July. Has Father William written anything for that month?"

Flicking through the pages, I stopped. "There's an entry here."

"Read it out," whispered Max, squeezing up tight to me so he could see the page.

8th July 2014

I stayed at the chapel late last night. I almost wish I hadn't. But then again, I wouldn't have been here to help those poor souls seeking refuge. Three volunteers came running into the chapel. I have never seen such distress. They could barely string a sentence together. I am horrified. Their arms are covered in black veins. Their fingernails like claws. They looked like they were dying. My head is still reeling from what they told me. Another drug trial had gone wrong. This confirms what Danny had told me in confidence. Middleton is running some kind of illegal drug tests in the old part of the hospital. I had no choice but to help them. I fear their life is in great danger. I wasn't sure if I would be able to get them past the security guards at the gate but I acted as a distraction. With all the commotion going on in the hospital, most of the guards had gone inside – looking for the volunteers I can only assume. I kept the guard at the gate talking while the volunteers slipped past. I have prayed to the Lord for their safety. I hope they take my advice and go to the bishop. I'm afraid for the young lady – Sylvia, I think her name is. She looked the worst. If the drug inside her doesn't kill her, then her mental state will. I can still see the terror behind her eyes.

I will go now. I have to go to the police in Holly Tree. I can't keep this to myself any longer. If it stops these dreadful drug trials from happening again, then it will be a blessing.

"The police," scoffed Max. "No wonder he's lying dead under that pew. I bet Inspector Cropper had something to do with his death."

"Maybe," I whispered. "We still don't know if one of those volunteers is your brother."

"Keep reading," urged Max. "I need to know."

I held the journal up and turned the page. I hoped for Max's sake that we would find some hope or clue that his brother had been one of those volunteers that Father William had helped to escape.

9th July 2014

I am scared. Scared for the volunteers. Frightened for my life. My visit to Holly Tree police station has left me alarmed. Warning bells are ringing inside my head. I don't understand. I told Inspector Cropper everything I have heard and seen at Cruor Pharma. He looked at me like I was nothing but an old fool. He tried to reassure me that Doctor Middleton was a great man – one to be respected. When I pushed him about the volunteers coming to the chapel, he told me I'd had a lucky escape. Said they were infected – they could have killed me. I told him they were infected with some drug but they weren't dangerous. He laughed. Told me they were wanted for the murder of seven other volunteers. I couldn't believe what I was hearing. I told him they needed help – his help. They aren't murderers – I know that. They're innocent. He wouldn't listen to me. I could tell he was getting angry. His voice almost broke when he shouted for me to leave the station and stop wasting his time. Now I am at a loss as what to do. I didn't tell Inspector Cropper that it was me who had helped them escape. I fear I will be in a lot of trouble if he finds out. What if Middleton finds out? What if they play back the tapes from the security cameras and see me at the gates? I must write to the Bishop. He will give me guidance.

I turned to the next page and carried on reading.

10th July 2014
Middleton confronted me about the escaped volunteers. He is evil. I am sure of that. When I say evil, I don't just mean a bad man. I mean evil as in some kind of dark force lives within him. He changed before my very eyes. The voice that spoke from him was not his. It was menacing. It told me things – personal things it couldn't possibly know about me. I am petrified. Never in my time as a priest have I seen such horror and wickedness. Never have I heard such hideous thoughts and threats. I held up my cross to him. Middleton's body jerked in front of me like he had been electrocuted. His face changed shape – he threw himself to the floor like he was fitting. I ran from his office. I was chased. Not by Middleton. I don't know what it was? A black shape – a dark mass. It followed me across the grounds. I prayed I would make it back to the chapel before it reached me. I didn't. The pain through my body is excruciating. I don't know what it's done to me? I feel as though my insides are burning.

God gave me the strength to crawl back inside the chapel – my sanctuary – they cannot follow me in here. I will recite the bible – it will give me comfort. I know now what evil lives amongst the walls of Cruor Pharma. I know what resides within Doctor Middleton. He is possessed. A demon has taken him.

I feel I have failed. I must have faith. I must pray for Sylvia, Alex, and Robert. I will speak to God – pray my letter reaches the bishop and hope they reach the safety of his parish. Maybe someone will find my journal and do the right thing for the volunteers.

I think I'm dying... I am in the chapel... I believe these will be my last words...

CHAPTER TWENTY FIVE

I closed the journal. "Demons," I whispered. "Father William describes Middleton just like Carly had been in that room."

"And he mentioned Robert," smiled Max. "My brother did escape. But where is he now? Why didn't he come and find me?"

"Perhaps he's on the run," I said. "He would've needed to get away from here as quickly as possible. Inspector Cropper told Father William that the volunteers were wanted for murder. No one's gonna hang about when they're wanted by the police. It's just the same as what's happening to us now. We're getting framed for the murders of Nurse Jones, the other volunteers, and now Fred Butler."

"I guess," sighed Max. "At least I know he got out of this hell-hole, but where do I go from here? How am I gonna find him? Did he make it to the Bishop?"

"I don't know?" I whispered. "I have no idea where the bishop lives. We know Sylvia didn't make it. She's locked up in some mental hospital. We can't look for Robert until we get out of here, but when we do, I'll help you." I looked down at my hand and wondered what Robert looked like now. Had he turned into some kind of monster? Is that why he hadn't come back for Max?

Max smiled. "Thanks, Kassidy."

"Poor Father William", I murmured, "He must have felt so helpless, so alone. So scared."

"If *he* couldn't deal with demons, I don't fancy our chances against them," said Max, standing up. "I'm gonna check on Jude, it must be time for us to go soon."

I sat quietly on the pew. If Middleton had a demon inside him and so did Carly, then Ben must be the same. But there were differences. Carly had seemed so out of control, whereas Middleton and Ben seemed able to come across like any other men, until you scratched deep enough and saw what really lurked under the surface. Could I trust Ben? Was it the real Ben who had helped me, or was it the demon in him? I had no idea.

I placed Father Williams's journal back inside the satchel. I would take it with me. If I didn't, I couldn't ever imagine anyone coming across it. It would lay undiscovered – slowly rotting with Father Williams's body.

"Hey, Kassidy," called Max from the doorway. "Jude's outside, he's feeling a little better."

"Good," I stood up. "I'll wake Raven."

I tapped her on the shoulder. Raven opened her eyes slowly and stared at me in a trance-like state.

"You won't be *you*," she hissed, backing away from me. "You're gonna change… I feel sick."

She pushed past me and stumbled out of the chapel. I followed after her, anxious to know what she meant.

"Raven, what do you mean…?" I stopped. She had her hand up against the chapel wall and was throwing up.

"Not another one sick," groaned Max. "I thought we were good to go, what with Jude feeling better now."

"She'll be all right," said Jude. "A bit of fresh air will do her good. The smell in the chapel probably got to her. What the fuck was that stench?"

"The priest," I said. "He's dead. His body is rotting under one of the pews."

"Shit," said Jude. "This place really likes its corpses. How many more are we gonna find?"

"No more, I hope. I've seen enough," I said, placing the strap of the satchel over my shoulder.

Raven straightened up. She wiped her mouth with the back of her hand. Her eyes wandered from Max to Jude, then stopped on me.

"Something horrible is gonna happen to *you*," she spat, her finger pointing accusingly at me.

"What the fuck are you going on about now?" snapped Jude. "Nothing horrible is gonna happen, we're gonna get out of here, get my car, and get pissed."

"Pissed?" said Max shaking his head.

"Yeah, I need a fucking drink after this vacation," huffed Jude. "This has been one hell of a night. I feel like I've been here for an eternity."

"We all feel like that," I said. "But getting *pissed* isn't gonna help us."

"We need to stay sharp. Once we get to your car, we have to get away from Holly Tree as quickly as possible," said Max.

"Fine – fine," said Jude, holding his hands up as if to surrender. "We can get pissed later – I can wait."

"Do you feel all right now, Raven?" asked Max. "We can't hang around any longer. We need to start heading toward the gates if we're leaving with the staff."

She nodded her head, peering out from under her black, straggly hair.

"What's the plan then?" she asked.

"We go out in twos," said Max. You go with Jude, I'll go with Kassidy. We've got two I.D. badges. Jude will hold his up and I'll show mine.

When we get out of the gates, we head down the path on Strangers Hill toward Holly Tree."

"Hang on, Max," I interrupted, "We can use the money we found in the bottom of Father Williams's satchel. There's enough for us to catch the bus. We can save a lot of time if we do that."

"It means travelling with the rest of the staff from Cruor Pharma, I don't know if that's such a good idea," said Max. "What do you two think?" He looked at Raven and Jude.

"What are they gonna do to us?" said Jude. "Even if they do suspect us, we're all stuck on a bus. And besides, it will probably be full of just porters, kitchen staff, and lab techs. Security won't be leaving here until they find us, so we don't need to worry about them."

"I think we should do it," I said. "As long as we act natural and spread out, then we'll just look like staff travelling home."

"I don't care how we do it," shrugged Raven, "I just want to get out of here. I'm not gonna feel safe until we're inside Jude's car and leaving Holly Tree."

"Okay then, the bus it is," agreed Max. "You'd better sort out the money now, Kassidy. We won't be talking to Jude or Raven when we get to the front of the main building."

"Ask for a single ticket to Holly Tree bus terminal," I said, handing out the coins. "Me and

Max will follow you two when we get off the bus."

"Make sure you hide that love-bite that Carly gave you," winked Jude, taking a handful of my hair and pulling it over my shoulder. "And don't forget to keep your claws hidden."

I looked down at my nails. I would have to make sure I kept my hand tucked into the pocket of my jacket. At least it was still foggy and there was no wind to blow my hair away from the bite-mark. I still had dried blood down my legs, although much of it had come off now. I bent down and spat onto my hand, scrubbing away at my skin. There was so much to remember. That feeling of dread was creeping through me – eating me up. I could feel that nervous tremor gorging on my insides. I didn't want to walk through those gates, but there was no other option.

"Okay, I think we're all ready to go," said Jude, turning toward the path in the direction of the hospital.

"We've just got to hope that the security guards won't bother to ask you two for your I.D.," said Max, running his fingers through his hair.

"What if they do?" asked Raven.

"We run," I whispered.

CHAPTER TWENTY SIX

We walked in silence. The fog had become patchier, allowing us snippets of what lay ahead. Our footsteps crunched on the gravel path as we followed it back up the side of Strangers Hill toward the main building. The lights from Cruor Pharma shone through the fog giving the early morning an eerie tone.

Up ahead, I could see the first dribble of staff leaving the main entrance and heading toward the security gates. Panic filled me. How would we mingle amongst such a small amount of people? I had hoped there would be large groups of staff all desperate to get home that we could hide amongst. This wasn't how I had envisioned it.

"Just hold back for a minute," whispered Jude. "We need to time; this just right."

We crouched down under the canopy of a small tree. Watching. Waiting. The security gates started to open, screeching through the fog on dried-up hinges. A line had formed by the gates with staff waiting to be cleared to leave. I strained my eyes trying to count how many security guards were manning the gate. I could see four. Two were checking I.Ds of staff leaving, and another two were letting the day shift through. A second gate had been opened allowing staff arriving by car access through to the car park. Each car was stopped, I.D. checked by another four security guards.

"There's more staff leaving now," whispered Max. "Come on, let's go." He pulled me up. "It's now or never."

I looked back at Jude and Raven.

"See you on the other side." Jude winked at me. "We'll hang back, give you a few seconds' head start."

My heart was racing. I stumbled forward. "Slow down, Max," I said. "We need to act casual. Keep the same pace as the rest of the staff."

He nodded his head. "Sorry," he breathed. "I feel like I'm gonna shit myself." He tried to smile but it looked more like a grimace.

"Me too." A nervous giggle slipped through my lips. I breathed deeply, every part of me on edge. Checking over my shoulder, I could just make out Jude and Raven. They had stood up and were now walking slowly toward the main entrance, just a short distance from us.

A large group of people stepped out from the doors in front of me and Max. It had started to get busy. The staff on day shift had started to crowd up outside the doors, pushing their way through the exiting staff. Max and I shoved through the crowd, positioning ourselves in the middle. I kept my gaze to the floor, fearful of making any eye-contact with the staff, just in case they looked at me and didn't recognise me to be one of them.

Keep your right hand hidden in your pocket – hair over shoulder to cover bite-mark – keep to Max's left – away from the security guards – act natural. I kept telling myself this over and over again. I couldn't fuck up. There was so much to remember. I could feel the heat creeping through me as I started to sweat. My hands felt sticky. Clammy. My neck damp. Fear started to overwhelm me. Act natural. *Act natural* the voice inside my head kept shouting.

"Did you hear what happened to Fred Butler?" a man in front of me asked the lady walking beside him.

She nodded her head. "They still haven't found those volunteers, the ones who killed him."

I glanced at Max. His eyes briefly met mine and then looked away.

"Better not let security on the gates hear you talking about it," piped in a man dressed in grubby overalls, the word *Maintenance* printed across the back of his uniform. "What goes on in here stays in here – remember?"

The lady nodded her head and carried on walking. I glanced up. How much further until we reached the gate? I couldn't see past the staff in front of me. I wanted to look behind. How far back were Jude and Raven? Had anyone stopped them? *Just keep your head down and keep walking,* that voice ordered inside my head. I nervously played with the coins inside my jacket pocket. My left hand gripped the satchel with such force my knuckles had gone white.

"Excuse me." I felt a tap on my right shoulder. *Shit. Keep walking. Don't stop*, I told myself.

"Hey." Another tap to my arm. Someone leant in between me and Max.

I turned my head a little, afraid to catch their gaze. Afraid I had been caught.

"You dropped this." A young man with ginger hair waved a folded piece of paper in front of my face.

The photo of my dad flapped open. I snatched it. Then started to panic when I realised I had used my hand, the one I had been desperately trying to remember to keep hidden. Shoving the photo into my pocket, I looked ahead.

"Thanks," I mumbled and continued to follow the crowd.

"Are you all right?" The ginger-haired man lightly gripped my arm. "You don't look well".

"I'm fine," I nodded my head. *Please go away. Stop talking to me. Leave me alone,* the voice inside my head pleaded.

"Long shift, eh?" he continued to talk to me. "These night shifts are killers. What department do you work in? I don't think I've seen you before."

"Look, mate," Max turned on him suddenly. "She's my girlfriend. She ain't interested in you, now fuck off and leave her alone."

"Hey, sorry, man, I didn't realise." He held his hands up and stopped walking, the crowd swallowed him up.

"Come on," whispered Max, pulling me nearer to him. He let out a big sigh, the stress getting to him.

The crowd suddenly came to a stop. We had reached the gates. The staff stood in a large bundle, all trying to push in front of one another.

"*Come on*," shouted a member of staff. "I've got a bus to catch."

I stretched up on tip-toes. Were they checking each I.D. badge individually? It looked like it.

"They're gonna ask me for my I.D.," I whispered, looking at Max. "What do I do?" My voice trembled. I felt sick.

"Blag it," whispered Max.

"And say *what*?" I mumbled, afraid that someone might hear me.

"Tell them you've lost your card," hushed Max. "It might work."

I stretched up on tip-toes again. Twelve more people in front of me. It would be my turn in just a few minutes. I felt faint. My heart beat like it was on a life support machine on speed. I chewed my lip. Swallowed down the scream that wanted to escape my throat. Ten more people to go. The line was getting shorter.

I reached up, grabbing a handful of hair and pulled it over my shoulder. What else? My mind was in a frenzy. Max's left side. That was fine. Hand. *Check your hand!* screamed the voice in my head. I thrust my right hand deep into the pocket of my jacket. I looked ahead. Six more people in front. Stay calm. Act natural. What if they check Max's I.D. card? They'll read the name – Fred Butler. Shit. Shit. Shit. This isn't gonna work. Four more staff in front.

"Stop Cruor Pharma from testing on animals – animal cruelty should be stopped."

I looked over at the gate. A large crowd of people holding up banners had swarmed around the entrance stopping the staff from entering and leaving.

"It's not science, its animal cruelty," the crowd shouted.

The two security guards at the entrance gate tried to hold them back but the group pushed forward chanting even louder.

I looked back at the line in front. Two more people were ahead of me and Max.

"Wait here," the guard on the gate ordered. He left the exit and walked over to the animal protesters who were still gathering outside the front gate.

I could hear the staff behind me grumbling about missing their bus. The two people in front looked at their watches, feet tapping impatiently.

I looked back at the security guards. They had their hands full, attention caught up with the protesters.

Turning to face Max, I said, "Let's go."

He nodded his head. We pushed past the two staff in front, hoping we wouldn't get noticed by security. The staff tutted at us as we shoved passed them and out through the gate.

Relieved to be out of the grounds of Cruor Pharma, I breathed in deeply. Would Raven and Jude be as lucky as me and Max?

The crowd had become more vocal. They thrust forward, waving and swinging their banners about. I turned to look at Max but got swamped up by the protesters. I tried to push through them. Their bodies tightly compacted around me. Each step forward I took, I was thrust back several paces. It was like being caught up in a wave and trying to swim against it.

"Please can you let me through?" I tried again to break across the crowd. My plea went unheard. The protesters were shouting and screaming, my voice lost amongst their cries. I couldn't see Max. Had he made it through the crowd?

Another shove back. I could feel the panic rising in me as I realised that I was now back within the grounds of Cruor Pharma – pushed back through the gates. I *had* to get out. I shoved back – using my shoulders to barge past two protesters. I collided with a man who stumbled back. He regained his balance. He stared at me.

"Scum," he spat. "Animal killer". He lifted his wooden banner and brought it down on my head.

I fell back. The protesters became nothing more than a spinning blur as my head hit the concrete ground.

"Get back!" A male voice screamed behind me. A pair of hands slipped about my waist and lifted me off the floor. I watched hopelessly as I was dragged away from the yelling crowd and back amongst the staff of Cruor Pharma.

"No," I protested, snatching at the hands that gripped me. I was being pulled inside a room. "I need to go." My head was still spinning. I tried to focus.

"You ain't going anywhere, missy. Not while those protesters are out there."

I looked up. My head pressed against the stomach of a security guard. He hoisted me up into a chair.

"You've had a nasty knock to your head." He walked around from the back of the chair and crouched down in front of me. "How you feeling?"

"Dizzy," I murmured, lightly touching the top of my head. I couldn't believe I was back within the grounds of Cruor Pharma. I'd had a few steps of freedom only to have it snatched away.

"Gonna have to fill out an accident form," he said, standing up and pulling open a drawer.

My eyes shot toward the door. There was no way I was going to hang about to fill out some crappy form. I had to get out. There was no time to waste. I looked back toward the open door. The crowd had grown. The protesters were shoving forwards, the security guards struggling to hold them back. Staff were piling up. Some shouting at the protesters. The noise was deafening.

"Here we go." The security guard turned around, holding a sheet of paper up. He grabbed a chair and placed it in front of me. Sitting down, he pulled a pen out from his shirt pocket. His name badge glinted from under the single bulb that hung from the ceiling - *Charlie*.

I stood up. "I haven't got time for this, I'm going home." I made for the door.

Charlie jumped up from his seat, quickly blocking my escape. "You ain't leaving till you've filled this form out, missy," he spat. "I ain't getting the sack for some silly girl who doesn't abide by the rules."

I tried to step around him. "I'll fill one out tonight when I come back for the night shift."

"No, you won't. You'll do it now," he ordered, his arms out-stretched on both sides, herding me back toward the chair.

Over his shoulder, I could see the gates had been pulled shut. The security guards leaning all their weight up against them, desperate to keep the protesters from breaking through. Their angry screams and chants pierced the air.

"I'm not filling that *shitty* form out now – I'm leaving," I snapped. I went to duck under his arm. He was too quick. He grabbed me by the shoulders, forcing me down onto the chair. Panic filled me. I had to get away. I had to find the others before they got on the bus. "*Get your fucking hands off of me – don't touch me!*" I screamed, shoving him back. I no longer cared if I didn't act like a member of staff. All that mattered now was my escape.

Charlie's eyes narrowed. "Where's your I.D. badge?" He loomed over me. His eyes filled with suspicion.

A voice suddenly sounded over his radio. "*Get your arse out here, Charlie – they're climbing up the gates.*"

"*You*," he pointed his finger in my face. "You, stay right there – *don't move*." He turned and ran out through the door.

I leapt up. If I was gonna escape then it had to be now. Slipping the strap of the satchel over my head, I charged out into the crowd.

CHAPTER TWENTY SEVEN

I was tangled up amongst the staff. Boxed in from all directions. I couldn't move. I stood on tip-toe, straining to see over the heads that bobbed about in front of me. My eyes shifted frantically from left to right through the wire fencing. Where were the others? I couldn't see them. Had they left me? Were they already on the bus? The protesters blocked my view. Their faces pushed up against the fencing like a pack of wild animals trying to break in. I tried to push through.

"Excuse me." I struggled to separate the two people stood in front of me. I pushed my arms out between them, hoping I could lever them apart. I didn't care if they saw my claws. I didn't care about anything other than escaping. They didn't hear me. The shouting and screaming had turned into more of a roar. I could hardly hear myself think. I had to get through. I charged forward, breaking past the block of staff only to find another barrier of people to get past. I pushed and shoved. I was gonna get out – even if I had to fight my way out. I rammed my way between the staff. The wire fence was closer now. The angry faces of the protesters screamed and swore. The security guards yelled back, their arms outstretched, trying to hold the fencing up from the weight of the protesters. How was I going get over the fence? The gates were shut and the fence lined with more than ten security guards. Even if I did try to climb it, I would be dragged back down by security. My eyes suddenly fell upon Jude and Max. They stood amongst the protesters, pulling and hanging on the fence. The sight of them spurned me on. I could do this. I elbowed my way through the staff, knocking them aside. Adrenaline giving me strength to propel my way forward.

"*Kassidy, over here!*" shouted Max. He pushed on the fence.

Jude leapt up, hooking his fingers into the wire. This was it. I was going over the fence.

I tried to push past a woman blocking my way. She wouldn't budge.

"*Move!*" I screamed at her. She ignored me. I grabbed a clump of her hair, desperate to get by her. I yanked her back. She fell to the floor – stunned. I clambered over her – my way now clear.

"*Murdering bitch!*" screamed one of the protesters as they saw me break through the staff.

I hesitated. The protesters' attention was now on me as I stood apart from the staff of Cruor Pharma. Their crazed faces leered at me.

They wanted my blood. If only they knew what really went on inside Cruor Pharma. There were no animal tests in there. Just humans. Victims like me.

I looked to the right. Charlie was screaming into his radio. Our eyes met.

I didn't need to think too hard. Cruor Pharma or the protesters? I ran for the fence.

"Oi, you," screamed Charlie, fixing his radio to his belt and charging toward me.

I ran. My legs moved liked pistons. My arms thrust me forward. I lunged for the fence. My fingers hooked onto the wire. I yanked myself up. My heart beat from within like it wanted to escape from my chest. My muscles burnt as I tried to pull myself up. My feet slipped from the fence and I hung momentarily as I tried to find a gap in the wire for my feet to prop on to.

"*Come on, Kassidy*," screamed Jude, his face just inches from mine as we clung onto the fence from opposite sides. His blue eyes filled with panic as he saw Charlie reach up and grab my ankle.

I slipped. Charlie's hand held me down – preventing me from climbing up. The protesters joined in. They shoved at the fence, knocking me, snatching at me. I hung on. Jude kicked out at them. His foot caught one of the protesters in the face. The man fell to the side.

"*Kick him off, Kassidy!*" yelled Max, his eyes on Charlie.

I looked down. With my free leg and my fingers gripping tightly to the fence, I kicked out. My foot smacked hard into Charlie's face. He stumbled back. I reached up. One of my shoes fell to the ground. My toes squeezed into a gap between the wire and I lifted myself further up the fence. Jude had climbed higher. His arm reached over the top of the fence, his fingers snatching for me.

"*Come here*," snarled Charlie, "I ain't letting you get away. I know who you are." He was back on his feet and climbing up under me.

The fence started to move. I could feel myself swaying backward and forward. The weight of the protesters throwing themselves against it was too much. I stretched out my arm. Desperate to feel Jude's fingers take my hand. The briefest touch of his skin against mine vanished as the fence came down.

I landed on my back. Stunned. The wire fence pinned me down. The protesters charged forward. They had forgotten me now as their break-in had been achieved. They clambered over. I had to get out from under the broken fence or I'd be crushed for sure. Jude and Max were trying to lift it up but the protesters barged through them, sending them flying. I could see

Charlie. He was trapped. Caught up in the broken wires. I used my feet to push myself back, sliding out from under the fence. I held my arms up as the protesters swarmed through the broken gap, charging in like frenzied animals. Staggering to my feet, I was knocked from left to right, my limbs tangled up with rushing bodies of the protesters and staff colliding as one. The noise was overwhelming. I wobbled forward, teetering on the broken fence. It lay at an awkward angle, broken banners strewn across it. Charlie still kicked about underneath the fence, half his body still caught up in the wires. I spun around. I had lost sight of Jude and Max. Which side of the fence were they on? Shaking, I moved forward, my escape out of Cruor Pharma right in front of me. I just had to get past the crowds.

"You ain't going anywhere." Charlie's voice filtered through the screams and shouts. He snatched at my ankle. I toppled over, landing on my knees.

"*Fuck off!*" I screamed, swinging my leg out as he pulled me toward him. The heel of my foot crunched down on his nose.

"You little bitch!" he bellowed, grabbing hold of my other ankle – dragging me nearer to him.

I wasn't gonna let this piece of shit ruin my escape. Not now. Not after everything I had been through to get this far. I screwed my fingers tight into a fist and slammed it down between his legs. He cried out. His hands fell away from my ankles. Tears welled up in his eyes. He curled up on his side, screaming. I jumped up. Determined, I shoved my way through the oncoming protesters. Their cries and chanting hurt my ears. I continued to push ahead. Another sound stopped me dead in my tracks. The faint noise of sirens. As if snapping out of a daze, I barged through the gap in the fence. The police were coming.

CHAPTER TWENTY EIGHT

I ran through the crowd of protesters, looking for Max and the others. A bus rumbled off into the distance, disappearing into the fog. Where were they? I frantically searched through the protesters. What should I do? The sound of sirens was getting louder. There was no time to wait. I shouted out my friends' names. I spun around. I couldn't see them. There were too many people. Too much noise. I couldn't compete with the screaming and chanting.

Bright lights suddenly appeared over the crest of Strangers Hill from both sides. The loud wail of sirens filled the air. The foggy morning was suddenly lit up with flashes of blue. I turned away. Desperation turned to panic. My eyes anxiously veered from left to right. I pushed through the crowd. I wanted to hide, but I had to leave. I knew the police weren't here for me – but I was scared they might think I was one of the protesters – or worse, Charlie might want to press charges for assaulting him, and if that happened then I would fall back into the hands of Doctor Middleton. I couldn't wait for the others. I couldn't let myself be arrested. The sound of tyres braking cut through the chanting. I looked toward the road. Four police vans and one police car had stopped. The vehicle doors swung open. The blue lights continued to flash. The police came charging out. I was swamped by the sudden onslaught of protesters running from all directions – avoiding arrest. I struggled through the running bodies – frantically seeking a way out. I didn't know which way to run. The police had formed a human chain. They were herding the protesters back toward the fence, their shields held high. I had to get past them or risk being held along with the protesters. Shoving my way through the crowd, I saw an open space. The police hadn't quite shut the gap in the chain. I ran. My eyes fixed on that gap. Nothing else mattered. I smashed through the crowd – not caring who I knocked over. Everything seemed a blur. I was running a race. I had to be first. I hit the open space. If I was going to get caught it would be now. I ran alone. Standing out from the crowd of protesters – breaking my cover. That feeling of being chased spurred me on. The angry shouts and cries of the police and protesters blasting through my ears forced me to move. I kept going. My bare feet oblivious to the sharp stones and cold road they now pummelled against. Two bright lights suddenly came out from the fog toward me. A bus. It narrowly missed me as I swerved off the road and veered among the fir trees that

crowded the top of Strangers Hill. I ran blindly –
zipping past trees – avoiding low branches.
Patches of fog swirled around me as I rushed on.
I kept going – unsure if I were being chased – too
scared to look over my shoulder. I felt myself fall.
My foot slipped on a loose lump of rock. I
tumbled over – my ankle twisting to the side.
Landing face-first on a bed of fallen pine needles,
I rolled onto my back. Tilting my head forward, I
quickly checked the area, hoping that no one had
been coming after me. Strangers Hill seemed
void of all life. If it hadn't have been for the
distant noise of police sirens, I would have
believed I was in the middle of nowhere. I sat up.
My breathing heavy, I rubbed my chest. My heart
beat so hard it hurt. I glanced about nervously.
The hill was compacted with dense fir trees. The
sky couldn't be seen through the fog, and even on
a clear day you would struggle to see sunlight
through the tall trees. I rubbed my ankle. It felt
stiff. I knew it was going to hurt as soon as I
stood on it. I cursed. This was all I needed. It
would slow me down. Grabbing on to a tree
trunk, I pulled myself up. Leaning my weight on
my good leg, I checked around me. I had no idea
of my exact whereabouts on Strangers Hill. I
didn't even know if I were on the right side of the
hill to get down to Holly Tree. I was completely
disorientated. The fog didn't help. All I could see

was dark, murky shapes hiding in the mist. At least if I followed the hill down I would eventually come to the road which twisted its way around the hill. That was my best bet. Maybe I would get my bearings when I reached the road.

I cautiously placed my foot down – preparing for the pain. It hurt, but I wasn't going let it stop me from getting off this godforsaken hill. I may have escaped from Cruor Pharma, but I wasn't safe. Not yet. I staggered forward, gripping onto tree trunks, slipping every so often on the damp pine needles. It was eerily silent. I shuddered and checked over my shoulder. All clear as far as I could see. I carried on. My good leg had started to hurt. It ached from putting all of my weight on it. I was exhausted. I thought of my bed back in my flat. If only I'd stayed tucked up in there yesterday morning none of this would have happened. But it was too late to think about *ifs* and *buts*. I was trapped in this nightmare. I didn't even know what I was going to do. The plan to get to Jude's car seemed pointless now. The car was useless without Jude. Should I even be bothering with heading to Holly Tree? What would I do when I got there? Where would I go? Had the others even escaped from Cruor Pharma? I had to believe they had. I didn't want to think about being left on my own, on the run – looking like this. I stopped for a moment. My right hand still scarred with thick, black veins filled with VA20. My nails a cloudy-grey, long and curled. I could cover them with black nail varnish easily enough, but my hand? I couldn't live with gloves on permanently. I staggered on. I would go to Holly Tree, head for The Fallen Star where Jude had left his car. Hope that the others were heading there if they had managed to escape and hadn't been arrested. And then what? We would need to find out what VA20 was. What it was doing to us and if we could remove it from our veins. We would have to stay low, keep out of sight from the police and Doctor Middleton. We needed answers. But who would give them to us? Who could we trust? I thought of Father William and his journal. Demons. That's what he thought Middleton and Ben were. Yesterday morning I would have laughed at the very thought, but after everything that had happened, after everything I had seen, the idea seemed more real.

    I wondered how Doctor Middleton had kept all this secret. The staff seemed unaware of what was going on. Nurse Jones hadn't had a clue and Charlie and his mate, Steve, seemed unaware of the true horrors that were happening inside the hospital. They had only heard whispers – rumours. Neither seemed to really care as long as they were getting paid well. And besides, they believed it was us who had killed Nurse Jones, Fred Butler, and the other volunteers. They had no idea what Middleton, Wright, and Ben were all about. They just thought they were covering up another experiment gone wrong. Keeping up the good name of Doctor Middleton and Cruor Pharma so they could keep their jobs and good pay. I let my fingers slide over the photograph of my dad inside my pocket. Had he been the same? Had he happily worked for Cruor Pharma as long as he got paid? Had he known the true horrors that went on inside Cruor Pharma and kept its secrets? Is that why he had drunk so much – to blot out the nightmares and his own guilt? He had certainly done a good job of keeping his employment hidden from me. But why had he left? Was he sacked? Maybe he had found out what Doctor Middleton was up to and had left. Yes, that must be it. My dad had been a drunk but I'm sure he wouldn't have played along with messed up experiments that turned people into monsters. Still, that uneasy feeling that all was not quite right where my dad was concerned tore away at me.

  The pain in my ankle had got worse. I needed to sit and rest for a few minutes. I plonked myself down on a fallen branch. Making sure I was alone, I lent my head against the trunk of a tree. How much further until I reached the road? It felt like I had been walking down Strangers Hill forever. I looked back at the way I had come. I couldn't tell how far down I was. The fog was like a thick blanket.

My thoughts turned to Raven. I hadn't seen her with Max and Jude at the fence. Maybe she had already fled? After all, she had been pretty pissed off – pointing her finger at me, Max, and Jude. She still blamed us for persuading her to have the drug test. My heart thumped in my chest as I thought about what she had said to me back at the chapel.

Something bad is gonna happen to you.

What had she meant? How did she know? Something bad *had* happened to me. I wasn't sure if I could cope with anything more. And what about the strength Raven had shown in the locker room? That was unnatural, even Max and Jude couldn't lift a guy up by his throat and hang him in the air. Maybe it was because of VA20? Could I end up like that? I dropped my head into my hands. There were so many questions and no answers. I wished I could curl up into a ball and hide away forever. But that was a long way off from happening – if ever.

The sound of a branch snapping pulled me out of my daze. I looked up to where I had come from. I held my breath. My heart started to race. My eyes strained to see into the fog. Shadowy shapes seemed to lurk in the mist. I froze. My brain screamed at me to run, but my feet seemed glued to the ground. I listened. Still nothing. The shadowy shapes stayed frozen to the spot. They were just trees shrouded by swirls of fog. The snapping branch had probably just fallen from one of the trees – broken by last night's storm. Even so, it had scared me. I pulled myself up. That anxious feeling making me tremble. I had to get going. I hobbled down the hill. This time at a quicker pace. Fuck the ankle, I thought. I would be in worse pain if Middleton got his hands on me. I looked back over my shoulder every couple of minutes. I was sure I could hear something in the distance but I couldn't make out what it was. Facing front again, I came to a sudden stop. I had reached the road. Leaning cautiously out from the treeline, I peered left and right. The road was clear of vehicles. Silent, foggy, and shrouded on both sides with fir trees. If I followed it to the left, it would lead me down toward Holly Tree. I stepped out. It was hard work trying to walk through all the trees. If I stuck to the road then maybe I would reach the town quicker. I could always step back amongst the fir trees if a vehicle came by. I had only gone a few steps when I got that feeling of being watched. A shiver ran down my spine. I didn't want to turn around. I was scared to know what was there. I could hear a low rumbling coming from behind me. I took a deep breath and spun around. A black van had stopped in the middle of the road. Its fog lights cut through the gloomy morning. The exhaust pumped out thick, black clouds which churned and swirled amongst the patchy fog. It reminded me of the Cleaners and their shadowy forms. I felt for the cross in my pocket. I held it tight in my hand. Did the Cleaners ever leave Cruor Pharma? Surely not. You couldn't have them wandering around. No, I was just being paranoid. But who was in there? It wasn't a police van. I took a step back, scanning the treeline for a quick escape. The van rolled forward – slowly. The cloudy fumes from the exhaust drifted up like a black marble effect swirling in the fog. I stumbled back, knocking into a tree trunk. I gasped when I saw the words written over the bonnet of the van. *Cruor Pharma*. Shit. I spun around. No sooner had I taken my first step, I knew I would never be able to outrun the van. The pain in my ankle was too much. I looked over my shoulder. The van had moved closer. The windscreen was covered in dirt. Just a tiny gap for the driver to see out of. I staggered forward. The van crawled past me and stopped. I felt sick. Unable to move, I stood and waited – my eyes fixed on the van. All my strength and determination drained away like a plug had been pulled from me. I waited for the jury to step out from the van and give me my sentence. Was it going to be life or execution?

Whatever the decision, I wished that it would just be over with. I had tried so hard – come so far to get away from Cruor Pharma, but here I now stood. I had failed. The passenger door swung open, its creaky hinges sending shivers through me. I swallowed hard, blinking away the tears that had started to fill my eyes. I awaited my fate.

Nothing.
No Cleaners.
No Middleton.

A spark of courage seemed to wake me up. That human desire to survive raced within me. I wasn't going to get in the van. I had a choice. I was going to walk straight past that open door. Fuck Cruor Pharma. Fuck Middleton, and fuck the Cleaners. If they wanted me then they would have to fight me. I took a deep breath and started to walk. I passed the open door. My eyes fixed on the road ahead. I didn't want to see who was in there. As I cleared the van a voice made me jump.

"Get in."

I ignored it. I carried on walking, determined to show whoever was inside I had no intention of getting in willingly. The van rumbled as it crawled forward passing me again.

"You need to get in if you want to escape everyone who's after you. You'll never outrun them."

I turned sharply. I recognised the voice. Ben Fletcher. He peered out. His blue eyes fixed on me. He patted the seat next to him as if to entice me in. A smile spread across his lips.

"I'm here to help you, Kassidy," he said, stretching out his arm, offering me his hand.

I thought back to how Ben had been with me last night. One minute helpful, and then really angry, taking hold of me by the throat and slamming me up against the wall. Hot – cold – nice – nasty.

"You said you were evil. You said you weren't safe to be around," I whispered, taking a step back from the open door.

Ben let out a huge sigh and stared out through the windscreen. "I'm not safe to be around. But I'm offering you my help and if you don't accept it, they'll get you, take you, and then you'll be lost forever." He turned to face me again. His eyes had clouded over like the exhaust fumes that swirled up amongst the fog.

Ben's eyes sent warning bells rushing through me. From the short space of time that I had spent with him, I knew that look. I needed to get away from him.

"I'm going," I said, turning away from the van. "I need to find the others."

I had only gone a short distance when I heard Raven's voice call out. I swung around – searching the treeline. I couldn't see her.

Her voice cried out again. "Kassidy."

My eyes fell upon the van. Was she in there? No, she couldn't be. I stepped to the side. Maybe she was coming down the road from behind the van. I still couldn't see her.

"She's in here." Ben stuck his head out from the driver's window. "I picked her up further up Strangers Hill."

I started to walk back toward the van, reluctant to go back to Ben but relived that Raven had been found. Maybe she would know which direction Max and Jude had gone in. Something caught my eye. A movement among the trees. I glanced to the side. That distant sound I had heard earlier had crept nearer. Dogs. I could hear dogs.

"Hurry up," shouted Ben, "The police are coming. If you don't get in here then…"

"Then what?" I glared at him, trying to pick up pace. The urge to just run was overpowering. If only I hadn't twisted my ankle.

"You'll end up back inside Cruor Pharma," he muttered as I reached the van.

Not knowing if I was doing the right thing or not, I climbed in, slamming the door shut. The ripped leather seats creaked as I sat down. Ben slammed his foot down on the accelerator, the wheels span as he pulled away. I looked out the window. A pack of dogs were running down the side of the hill toward us, followed by a group of policemen. I clung onto the dashboard as Ben swerved the van tight around the sharp bends, throwing me from one side to the next. I came off the seat, hitting my head on the roof of the van as we dipped down into a pothole.

"Get your seatbelt on," Ben ordered as I slammed into him, knocking the gearstick.

"I'm trying," I snapped, as I was flung against the window. "Raven, I hope you're holding onto something," I shouted over my shoulder into the back of the van.

I felt dizzy. The van continued to spiral down. I reached for the seatbelt and clicked it shut. Looking to my left, I peered into the wing mirror. I could see Strangers Hill disappearing behind me. We were speeding along the road which led into Holly Tree. Cruor Pharma sat concealed behind a wall of stagnant cloud, hidden from view, hiding its evil secrets.

"Are you okay?" whispered Ben, taking his foot off the accelerator a little.

"I'm just hoping I never have to see that place again," I said, staring into the wing mirror. I turned to speak to Raven. A black curtain hung behind me, separating the back of the van from the driver's compartment. I pulled it open.

"Are you all right, Raven?" I began, but fell back into my seat – stunned. The rear of the van was empty. The floor was covered in blood. I looked at Ben. He turned. His eyes were that cloudy black colour again.

"I told you I was evil," he grinned, slamming his foot down on the accelerator.

I shot back in my seat, heart racing, scared at the thought of where Ben was taking me. What did he have planned for me? Was he going to be my protector, or killer?

BOOK TWO COMING SOON...

To connect with Lynda O'Rourke visit her facebook page at:

Lynda O'Rourke – Author

Printed in Poland
by Amazon Fulfillment
Poland Sp. z o.o., Wrocław